Praise for
2040: A Fable

"Incredibly thought-provoking"

"*2040* is incredibly thought-provoking. Bruce Piasecki wrote this masterpiece during the Covid19 pandemic and more importantly, during the year of his daughter's wedding. With a lot of emotions, he stepped away from his normal business management books and dwelled into today's societal impacts of technology and artificial intelligence on our daily lives. This well-written book is both thoughtful and entertaining."

—Sam Smolik

Author of *The Power of Goal Zero*,
former VP and SVP at Shell and Dow, current Board Member

"Thoughtful and absorbing"

"A thoughtful and absorbing read, with a message to the world.
Bruce Piasecki writes with energy and vision."

—Jay Parini

Author of *Borges and Me*, and of the bestselling film and novel
The Last Station, starring Helen Mirren

"Bursts of insight"

"Rich in humor and creative disruption, Piasecki's compelling
fable of turbulent times reveals a human wisdom.
His Felliniesque cast of characters share bursts of insight about life
in an age of surveillance capitalism."

—William Throop

Professor of Philosophy and Environmental Studies,
former Provost of Green Mountain College, book author

"Timely insights"

"Piasecki offers readers ten banners to live by. In twelve chapters we learn ten principles, including: eye contact and small talk with all, journaling, the need to 'investigate rather than simply download.' With its timely insights into social value, family, and friends, I heartily recommend this book"

—Rabbi Laurence Aryeh Alpern

Temple Shabbat Shalom, New York, United States

"A dark, funny, and searching rumination"

"Seeing Bruce Piasecki speak in Sydney, Australia, in 2012 awakened me to what can only be done through the careful crafting of ideas and a forceful narrative. The talk and his books taught me to avoid the primrose path of short-term thinking. That night, I resolved to apply to graduate school in New York and intern at Bruce's company. During that internship, I spent days in Saratoga, the setting for his latest book. Bruce captures the eccentricity and quiet beauty of his community surrounding the Old Stone Church, contrasting and connecting them to a world on edge, wound tight within a digital panopticon. A dark, funny, and searching rumination on our shared future."

—Sebastian Vanderzeil

Director of Strabo Rivers, Brisbane, Australia

"An amazing book"

"In *2040*, Bruce Piasecki provides sharp phrases you never see coming until they hit you on the head. He has done this since I first meet him over a quarter century ago, during his early pioneering work on business and society. Then, I stayed overnight one night a week to take his four-hour seminar on social and business change at RPI, where Dr. Piasecki was the founding director of a Master of Science degree at America's oldest engineering school. He still fascinates on the role of society and technology in nature. Here, in an unexpected fable, he notes the behavior of kingfishers, pileated woodpeckers, a peacekeeping owl, and a parrot to celebrate his sneaky insights. An amazing book. Read it with joy."

— Matthew Polsky
former New Jersey state official and author of *Overcoming Mind-Set Obstacles* (doctoral dissertation)

"Thought-provoking"

"Bruce Piasecki's fable presents one possible future, where the State and Tech combine to surveil society, drive obedience, and further erode the faltering line between public and private lives. In this Age of the Virus and climate consequences, government can impact the weather and even manipulate human memories. Yet, Piasecki offers us a sanctuary in Saratoga Springs, where family, friendship, and a renewed connection to the natural world provide hope and temporary respite from a turbulent world. This thought-provoking work will spur the reader to consider the consequences of today's choices on the world of 2040."

— Rick Goss
Principle, Green Cognition LLC, Washington, D.C.

"Stimulates important conversations"

"Bruce Piasecki's *2040: A Fable* is a powerful reminder of forces
that define our lives: environmental forces beyond our control,
where we must learn to survive, and other forces such as our choice
of friends, choice of neighborhoods, and choice of schools—
all within our control, and all determining our state of contentment.
This fable illustrates the bizarre and the serene and our need to adapt.
2040 stimulates important conversations."

— Bill Higgins
President & CEO, Saratoga Garlic Co.

"A cautionary tale"

"Piasecki uses his unique 'sportive seriousness' to entertain
us even while he pits the strength of human relationships
against the strange mechanisms of a surveillance state. Human ties win.
But *2040* is a cautionary tale we can ill afford to ignore
in an age of artificial intelligence and manufactured truths."

— L. Rostaing (Ross) Tharaud, Esq.
Attorney

2040: A Fable

Other Books by Bruce Piasecki

Dedication

To Andrea Carol Masters, my wife since college; and our lovely daughter Colette, her husband Sam, and my friends Scot Paltrow and Ross Tharaud, also from college. I thank Thaddeus Rutkowski for this meaningful introduction and retrospect; and Frank Weaver, who copyedited the MS and helped give shape to the published book.

Literary Dedication

To the long shadows of Mark Twain. We honor your Huck, Tom, Jim, and fake name. You stand tall in our Lotos Club.

2040: A Fable

by Bruce Piasecki

First published in 2021 by
Creative Force Fund

The Rockwell Kent woodblock print images reproduced throughout this book are from the limited Covici-Friede edition of Geoffrey Chaucer's *Canterbury Tales* (published in 1930) and used by permission of the Plattsburgh State Art Museum, SUNY Plattsburgh.

Ordering Information for Print Editions

Quantity Sales: Contact Awards@ahcgroup.com for discounted bulk orders over 10 units of any title done by Bruce Piasecki, including prior books. These rates go as high as a 50 percent discount for orders over 50 books; and the rate is dependent on the email request and intended use. Expect between 20 and 50 percent off list price.

Orders for Board or College Use: The founder of the Creative Force Fund, in seeking broad use of these books for Boards of Directors and the new generation of Business and Society users, offers an across-the-board discount of 30 percent for Board and School uses. Again, orders should be directed to Awards@ahcgroup.com.

print ISBN: 978-1-09837-418-1
ebook IBSN: 978-1-09837-419-8

Printed and distributed by BookBaby
www.bookbaby.com

Printed in the United State of America

10 9 8 7 6 5 4 3 2 1

2040
A FABLE

BRUCE PIASECKI

Creative Force Fund

2021

Table of Contents

Introduction

By
Thaddeus Rutkowski

College Years

I've known Bruce Piasecki since we were undergraduates at Cornell in the mid-1970s. We met in an advanced class focused on the works of John Milton. That class motivated me to read *Paradise Lost* in its entirety, and probably more than once. What impressed me about Bruce was that he wrote poetry and saw life in poetic terms. For Bruce, an ordinary intimacy, such as one between students, could inspire a poetic line, such as: "Your hands cling brownfully to mine." He spoke like this even back then.

Could this have been an early nod to diversity? Perhaps.

We both came to this elite school, looking sideways at the elites. Me, being raised by an Asian mother and Polish father; Bruce being raised by Polish parents, with a pure Polish grandmother, his Babcia, in his home from birth to Cornell. Bruce considers his experience interracial and multicultural, before those phrases became fashionable or even noticed in America, as he had foster brothers and sisters from Puerto Rica and Asia. We were odd men out in a blizzard of mostly male whites in faculty and the classrooms.

Bruce's accelerated course schedule inspired me to enter the dual degree program and graduate with a B.A. and a B.F.A in four years and a summer. Moreover, Bruce had the wherewithal to collect his poems into a book, *Stray Prayers*, published by Ithaca House press, before he finished undergraduate in three years. Bruce was studying at the pace of a high-speed car on an open highway, having been brought up, as he notes in his creative memoir, *Missing Persons*, in a home without newspapers and a prominent edition of the Bible in bare shelves.

On one occasion, Bruce brought me to the Ithaca House press, in a house in downtown Ithaca, where I offered my help as needed. I spent some time sorting movable type into appropriate slots in wooden trays. Bruce did the same; not knowing that someday he would write a bestseller, *Doing More With Less*, be elected to the Lotos Club by Tom Wolfe, while also being elected a member at the National Press Club for his books on business and society. As in his coursework at school, Bruce did not choose single paths; and like some characters in this book, he had a photographic memory on different subjects and passions.

During our years together in Ithaca, I was dimly aware that Bruce was a basketball player—what he called "my true love, the bounce of a round ball." This fun fact didn't lodge deeply into my mind until he had knee surgery, serious career-ending knee surgery. Afterward, I accompanied him to physical therapy in the Teagle Hall gym—this was our version of hanging out. I watched as he sat and flexed one knee to lift weights on a machine. I really had no idea of the excruciating nature of such therapy until many years later, when I fractured my shoulder and had to go through months of similar rehabilitation.

The Sportive Tone

After we'd headed in different directions to attend graduate school, I didn't see Bruce often. But I heard from him. I do remember one of his vivid visits to Baltimore, where my fan belt was fraying as he arrived at the train station. We made it back to my apartment in one piece. Bruce celebrated this turn of events as "shared Polish blind luck." He smiled as an affordable mechanic was not far downhill. We talked books and poems as we waited for a repair.

There was an occasion in Manhattan, where I had moved after graduate school at Johns Hopkins, when I heard Bruce read Biblical-style poetry in a private apartment. I remember his voice. I recall his friends then were doctors and lawyers and Native American chiefs. This performance may have been a tribute to the poetry of a great religious text Bruce was dreaming up, or simply an odd form of acknowledgment of spirituality of this still young writer.

In any case, I remember the sportively serious tone of all of his writing; his passionate conversations, and his focused reading regime. He clearly took life seriously, yet with informed and ironic distance. *2040: A Fable* embodies this world-view, which Bruce calls Polish essentialism. This "coming of age" tale shows how the protagonist, George, comes to a broader understanding of himself and the world in which he lives. In this way, the story line proceeds on classical literature patterns, like he was taught by M. H. Abrams.

Though we kept in intermittent touch, as our family obligations and work grew, I didn't see Bruce again until 2011. I drove a rented car from New York to the Vermont College of Fine Arts to appear on a literary-publishing panel. I stopped to visit him at his home outside of Saratoga Springs, the same neighborhood captured in this book. This entire experience was like a scene from the book before you.

Bruce greeted me in his driveway, where, at the street end, a car had crashed onto his property. He had greeted the drivers from the crash early that morning, flabbergasted and delighted that they had not died—as all three stood up before him, "as agile youth"—he noted, after leaving the seriously crushed vehicle. Bruce took this to mean something, but not something apocalyptic, simply something hilarious. Three soldiers had gotten drunk on gin, and crashed their vehicle into one of his large 200-year-old majestic maples. You could see the dent in the tree, "but it was a minor dent that did not touch the soul of the tree," Bruce had noted. He had a name for most of the large trees on his lawn.

I remember Bruce picking up the red fragments of the smashed head lights, tracing some of the fragments to their matching sisters all the way to the Stone Church across the street from his property. "Imagine how they sailed in the night," he said, laughing.

Throughout that day, we talked about writing, and about the nearby Yaddo colony, where I'd been in residence a couple of times without knowing that Bruce lived nearby. I saw Bruce's wife, Andrea, and Bruce's mother on that visit—family members who figure, along with other friends, teachers, and neighbors, into the book-length fable.

These people, and his imagined friends Abe and Winston, serve as foils for George in this narrative. George is the observer, the chronicler; while Abe is the warmhearted reporter; while Winston is the tax attorney. While you feel some echoes to Abe Lincoln and Winston Churchill in their discourse, clearly these people are actual extensions of persons Bruce knows well. This imaginative book is about his roommates, his lifelong wife, and his daughter, now married at twenty-five, extrapolated into the realm of 2040. These characters help George navigate the fog of his growing certainty that a kind of protest song is required for him to cope.

Crashing Into 2040

In this fable, Bruce Piasecki alludes to many of the themes I've mentioned—from crashing oddities to serious and solemn reflections on family, friends, and social needs. Twenty years from now, he still appreciates competitive basketball, though mostly as a passionate fan. In the fable, his favorite team is the Poles, who happen to share his heritage. He values friendship throughout his life, in the form of those same two people whom he met in college, Abe and Winston. And, of course, he values literature: the poetry of Chaucer and Whitman and Bob Dylan, among others. The story follows the lives of a married couple who live in upstate New York. Here Bruce tells how they've coped with changes in the world that have come about since our present time exploded. This is a work of world literature extrapolated into fable.

According to one definition, a fable is a story that conveys a moral.

In this book, there are numerous lessons about what is valuable (friends, family, and the freedom to work as one wishes). This ability to work as one dreams is well dramatized in the final parts of this book. There are also warnings about what can devalue our lives (a reliance on exclusive technological communication, a bowing to the ever-watchful State). As with all good fables, these lessons apply to all of us.

As with most speculative fiction, Piasecki is not writing about some strange future world; he is offering ideas, through metaphor, that apply directly to our present world. This remarkable projection to 2040 is absolutely a stunningly sustained technique to help us see through today.

Freedom Versus Fate

There is a sustained reflection on how one becomes themselves; this becoming is the key. I remember Bruce preoccupied with these questions of freedom and fate even while at Cornell. This fable is framed as a battle between thought and event. Piasecki has invested the time to make this book sing with alarm, warmth, and a genuine message of freedom in these times of simple lies. While similar to its sisters *Animal Farm* and *The Handmaid's Tale*, this *Fable* is a welcome exception to so much in modern literature that is excessively dark and limited.

Piasecki has offered us a large ocean's chambered nautilus shell, where you can hear in it what you bring to it, in addition to some remarkable passages of simple beauty and articulation. Piasecki has offered us a fable that both answers questions as it provides amusement and delight—so different in affect from Bruce's supercharged superhero of old, George Orwell. Bruce gives us this tale as a way up and out of the disasters of today.

Thaddeus Rutkowski is the author of seven books, most recently *Tricks of Light*, a poetry collection. His novel *Haywire* won the Asian American Writers' Workshop's members' choice award, and his memoir *Guess and Check* won an Electronic Literature award for multicultural fiction. He teaches at Medgar Evers College and received a fiction writing fellowship from the New York Foundation for the Arts. Visit his website at www.thaddeusrutkowski.com.

2040: A Fable

Part One:
Family First

Chapter One:
Divine Splendid Isolation

George was a reflective man, a thinking man.

George understood that winter is survived by the vain, the honest, the militant, the self-deceiving, the naïve, or the fragile and sincere. God was good to a range of peoples.

For George, life was all a magical battle between thought and event, truth and lies.

Yet winter remains hard on all types of humans, he observed, as evident each year in this neighborhood. Their survival was as much about luck and persistence as it was about likely selection or preservation of the saints. You may have strong first principles on how you run your family, enjoy your friends. You may believe in what matters.

Yet winter will test those principles like a tyrant.

The First Three Weeks of January

George would ready himself for winter with a pile of books near. Walt Whitman's self-absorbed charm; Emerson's smart rankings on freedom and fate; contemporary books since the 2030s, but only if they had something foundational to say about the human soul. He adopted, in winter, his mother's habit of cracking sunflower seeds to appease some of the anxiety found in his face and jaw.

Because George was raised poor, there was a quiet desperation in him. His Puerto Rican foster brothers taught him the better word *desperado*. It rhymed with tornado, so he felt it a more incisive word. To George *desperation* sounds too Ivy League, too much like the nose-in-the-air folks. *Desperado*—that is the word to describe George to date.

No matter how rich he became, not matter how secure, how much loved, he woke with the fears of Job, certain some new acquaintance was close to the devil. This unsteadiness came with his sense of the virtues and the vices. His wife, of Sicilian descent, could imagine a crown of thorns above his spine—and she would massage at night his weary neck, saying: "It must be hard, George, keeping up such a big head all day long." They would laugh together, ready to cuddle.

"You have a stupid mouth sometimes," Varlissima warned. He would think about that for a decade, and write a book about it. She encouraged him to do more and say less. Even though he tried to remain stoic, and silent, and listen to what others had to say, he had an irrepressible native exuberance in his bones. He was a reflective man, and less and less a stoic man.

Polish peasant-made people are sometimes like this. Feeling like he had ascended into a world far higher than ever imagined, it was hard for George to assume that mask of silence for long. By afternoon, after writing at his desk, he was the big mouth again. "Big shot, big shit," his grandmother warned many decades before.

Much went flying by in George's mind each morning, stimulated by fine coffee and captivity. Most of the scenes of his youth were so brutal they were over in thirty seconds; but the new George, the older George, could afford to ruminate.

Winter in Saratoga is relentless: icy, stern, long. The first three weeks of January stood still, completely frozen. Ice on all the lovely trees. Slender brittle branches of the younger ones snapped. Pools of black ice on driveways. Ice, shining in the afternoon sun of late January. This was all very strange, strange like the moisture and hot extremes of last summer. Weather patterns in 2040 were more volatile than world markets.

It causes some like Abe, a journalist in the immediate neighborhood, to get mean. It causes George's lawyer neighbor, Winston, to get philosophical and meaner.

It is almost comical, this distorting effect of winter. Abe once called Tony, another neighbor, "a violent and brain-dead servant of the State." Yet that was in a January, when most had sludge for brains.

The Origin of Self-reliance

Emotions change as the seasons change, and neighbors become more neighborly. You do not notice this truth, George noted, if you are merely self-reliant. It is in watching the odd pattern of loved ones, measured across the slightest variances, in journals, and in your head, when the truth emerges as a higher set of facts. Emotions change. The seasons change. Neighbors stay near.

This region's winters teach you self-reliance in the grandest American tradition. The need for self-reliance does not change as you age. Massachusetts, Vermont, New Hampshire, the Adirondacks—all icy. Those settling in Saratoga thought they might get a break from the longest of winters, being in the lower portions of the Adirondacks. Yet they were wrong. They were all part of the Northern Kingdom. "We hate the Big Eight in the winter," George wrote one night, leaving the details to stew.

In winter, you feel for your neighbors, family and friends, as reports of some falling on their asses increase, and as old folks break hips and the Saratoga hospital fills with these broken seniors.

February is when you really feel it. The shadows of each day are long. Memory can overtake experience, some days in winter.

You come to need neighbors, even if they proved mindless on several prior occasions. It is not about the warmth or intelligence of the conversation; it is about human contact.

The endless daily updates on the Virus infections worsened the emotions of winter. Spreading germs this winter made the feeling of isolation heavy for all, from the joys of children to the dreadful days of the elderly. There seemed to be no clear way forward, except to derive local warmth for the closest of near friends.

At his deepest self, George understood he and his family would prevail. Yet at times, it did seem as if he was skipping on a tightrope over a snake pit while juggling thousand-year-old Japanese Kamikoto knives.

Bursts of Dignity

Despite the horrible weather, Varlissima felt lucky to have the two closest, across-the-street neighbors, Tony and Allison. The quartet near the Stone Church assembled four very different and sonorous people. Allison appeared smart, and Tony was clearly important.

Varlissima felt warm towards them instinctively, well before they got to know each other. She felt it with her expressive Sicilian anticipatory warmth. "Hell," she thought, "if you are part of the neighborhood this long, you pass the test. We like you. Come on in." Her eyebrows and smile said the same.

George, a social historian, and her husband, cautioned Varlissima about getting too friendly too fast with these neighbors, saying: "My sweet

Varlissima, I get a sense from Allison that Tony is holding her like a wolf by her ears."

There was no proof of this. This was nothing short of pure instinct like a Biblical warning, as George was raised by a born-again mother, and tended to see deeply into the everyday. While Varlissima had bursts of dignity in her days, George was simply ruminating. His father had died early of a traumatic brain injury from war; and George was a thinker as a result. He wanted to think about everything in case he was cheated of life like his father. George said late one midnight: "Hey Varlissima! Please let us give Allison and Tony some time to thaw out before we jump into their lives."

A Pattern of Distance

For three long years, George and Varlissima watched an athletic Tony and an articulate Allison across the street, raking, planting explosively colorful Dutch hybrid bulbs, which suggested "Hello, come in." But the toxicity of 2040 had invaded our private lives, so caution prevailed. There might prove a peaceful volley of hellos and goodbyes between them, but nothing of substance. A pattern of distance prevailed.

Tony worked away often, and Allision stayed at home. Allison brought a dignified European feel to this patriotic American neighborhood. This calm prevailed in the Stone Church neighborhood, even though some were aware of the riots and protests in the streets elsewhere in the world.

Across these frigid winters, Varlissima and Allison talked about birds—from across a twenty-foot road—both being attentive birders. From diving ducks on the next-door pond, to cuckoos, and kingfishers, and dignified and insistent piliated woodpeckers—they compared notes across the street on bird citations most weekends. George found all of this warm and amusing, to have these two distinguished college-educated women standing across the street from each other, sharing bird notes.

Before the Age of the Virus, neighborhoods, no matter how poor or how rich, were like bathtubs, very large white bathtubs, where the natures of most people in the neighborhood were known, as they all shared the same water. But these days were days of relentless downloads and hidden secrets.

Like a rare eagle thinking herself a minor hawk, Varlissima seldom disappointed the neighborhood. She was known as the Bird Queen, even in winter. Over time neighbors gave Allison the nickname "The Book Queen." Both names stuck as obvious as a smear of an insect's wings on a car windshield.

We all had nowhere else to go because of the pandemic. George and Varlissima felt Allison and Tony orderly, lovely, kind, and attentive. Yet a dusty pattern of distance kept them remote from their closer selves.

Dignity at a Distance

George was a pensive man, walking around the neighborhood. The hours of early morn were his best. "The hours of the wolf," he called them, alert and strong. He sported a cap, a beard worthy of a monk, and often walked gingerly and slowly into the afternoon owing to his old basketball knees. He knew each contour of his region well.

This part of Saratoga may not have changed all that much since the famous Battle of Saratoga in the 1770s, the battle that set the American rebels free of England. George called this "changeless terrain, and thereby, sacred terrain." It had many farms, open valleys, old distinguished homes, and a few businesses and restaurants.

Kayaderosseras Creek kept stability in this place of reverence; the K Creek's languid lands offered mist and calm, fleeing turtles and plenty of beautiful birds. As a guide to the perplexed, and the idle, the Creek offered access to herons and rails, diving birds of no spectacular splendor or name, and even flycatchers. A few floating pigeons could make an afternoon. But all of this was a distant memory during the frigid winter.

The Creek was frozen now, and would stay that way until April. Yet it was easy to walk by it; or drive by it, and remember warmer days. Along the creek, George Washington had camped before the Battle of Saratoga, a mere two miles down the trail from the Old Stone Church neighborhood. This was historic, as well as sacred, in George's mind.

The steady running creek, what the veterans of the area called K Creek, kept running—George watched, hands folded, as its shaded and good head of water drops and turns and twists and drops again as all old creeks do. George knew its rhythms and its peace. This was his special Kayaderosseras Creek, a strong proud American creek, running like the small and larger gods of ancient Greece.

The neighborhood was far inland, and hard to change despite the racial riots and police violence elsewhere. The thing George loved about the creek was that it held no grudges. Like a god, it never demanded revenge.

It was a peaceful, powerful creek, worthy of admiration.

This creek reminded George that he too would pass, like the other characters occupying his life, but that this glorious lonely creek would continue to flow.

He found peace in that thought, despite the turbulence around.

Chapter Two:
They Dine with Their Neighbors

Even though it was still only February, both the men and women of this neighborhood could anticipate a time when you could clean up the mess made by the passing trucks. "Soon enough we will be outside again; let's plan for the spring cleanup now," Varlissima said to Allison.

One of the many delights that Allison brought across from England was an annual spring street cleanup. During these idle days cleaning up our neighborhood, Allison would say such brilliant things as:

Of the 100 greatest books, the greatest is Petronius' Satyricon. You may ask why? Well, let's first think why the Italian Fellini brought it back to life in a recent movie. It is because these are universal types. Petronius knew these types that remain to this day! In our neighborhood. There are many great ghosts in his book, walking around to disturb our peace today. I agree the Fellini movie is full of disgusting things, but such is life. We live with the ghost of my mother each day, and that is wonderful. Life is like this, a pile of bad people and cluttered things. You can always clean up the mess. Every time my wondrously informed husband and I turn on our computer for political discussions, we see Petronius staring at us, with his bent smile, from the clouds! The world is such a disorderly mess. Let's clean it up. Carry on, chaps.

"It was easier to think about the garbage on our streets than Petronius, frankly," noted Abe one morning during breakfast at George's home, reflecting on the past clean-up. Varlissima echoed in agreement; it was hard enough to keep one's house clean, find safe food, and enjoy a few good movies.

The breakfast at George's proceeded as usual with Abe and Winston; and with constant chatter about their neighbors. Abe and Winston joked about how Allison was actually thinking about her own mortality when she raised her mother from the dead.

Prejudice Is Like a Stone in a Child's Shoe

In time, even in winter, every neighborhood needs an inspiring coach like Allison to rally the troops. Allison would continue on as our coach. We accepted that. We even accepted how she'd rattle on about that ancient Roman farce-maker, Petronius.

Allison joked that some of the names on the block were "as hard to pronounce as Petronius." She was referring to the non-Anglo immigrants down the block, in the trailer park. This fundamental prejudice in her mind was like a stone in a child's shoe. She kept walking with it. She did not need to encounter actual splinters in her path, for the fracture existed already in her head. "Nothing you can do about it," noted Abe.

To her British transplant standards, "These Russian transplants did not have enough when it came to gardens, and they left a good deal of garbage on their lawns." This was the ugly side of Allison, how she filed thoughts out loud. All this came out, all these slings and arrows about immigrants, even before George and Varlissima really were invited in.

We participated in this neighborhood cleanup tradition for years, a regimen aligned with gentle purpose, and little self-reflection. It did not matter that people were dying all around the nation. "With a nudge here, and a nudge there," Allison noted, "we can keep our world on course." It became a neighborly mantra by 2040.

It was all very comical, and useful, noted both Abe and Winston. These graduate-level literature cleanups served us well as we waited for more time outside. The Bureau of State Security gave us points for listening to Allison; as if she would single-handedly keep some of the barbarians behind our gates.

We were in a neighborhood of rare calm, and it was simply easy to remain there. Sometimes, rare statements of prejudice were overlooked by the citing of a single owl between the residences. While legal process may be a way to teach the prejudiced social justice, it is a very slow, expensive process. Easier to be distracted by the flick of an owl's brow. We were not so much expecting barbarians as we were waiting for some relief.

The Deeper Past of Allison

February has a way of reminding all of the proximity of death to life. It is a blow to the stomach that outlasts the chill of a good film. February is God's way of teaching humility in Saratoga.

Our neighborhood was still frozen by the end of February, but winter was beginning to lose her grip. You could anticipate it. It paid to anticipate it. Before the pandemic, Varlissima and George would fly to Arizona to shorten the wait for spring; but now they discussed classics and bird behavior.

As soon as a first hint of spring was smelt, Allison got booties on and fitted plastic protectors on each of us, and led two dozen neighbors, including their teenagers, down the street "to rid it of debris." Time for cleanup rehearsals!

Varlissima noted that what fell under Allison's term "debris" was comprehensive—an endless stream of gin bottles and hamburger wraps that pop up alongside every country road in the States. Toast would not count, that was "for the birds." You could bypass anything organic, in fact. It was the left-over plastics that outraged. We rehearsed the lists for clarity of purpose well before the actual cleanup days.

On the day itself, tradition again is most likely to prevail. Allison would come back to stand before her fine home with handfuls of tiny cigarette butts that never seemed to biodegrade. This was the source of Allison's concentrated focus this cleanup, and a polite one at that—cigarette stubs were each condemned with British aristocratic abandon.

Birds could be accepted, immigrants questioned, but the debris of any human remained her target during spring cleanup. She collected from the rich neighbors and the trailer parks. She was the universal spring cleaner.

Nobody told anyone regarding this feature of Allison. Everyone just knew. In a mere month or two it would be spring again, and Allison would be rattling us with classic thoughts and good deeds again.

Yet when you click on your computer, things can change and pivot in a matter of seconds. This is what added elements of hysteria to the politics of the extended pandemic.

It took a few days at our computers in early March, but the storyline was clear: our Cleanup Heroine had a checkered past. It started with the projection of this image from her past, when she was both monkish and British, serious, and so solemn. It was clear by the set of downloaded pictures that sunny Arizona had been good for her; but those days in Manhattan became checkered. Allison had been a Manhattan literary agent, where she came to the city from London. Most of what she sold was lovely, indeed, but some of it was ugly.

The memory machines then started sharing a few of her more famous refrains, in a sequence that had dramatic mounting music behind it. It started with one of her famous refrains:

> *Were it not for my lovely stepmother, I would still be on the wrong side of that dark, dark London, where it rains on Monday, pours on Tuesday, and you can hardly see through the fog each weekend.*

Whatever sparked thoughts of her Mom, this reminder of her sensual dislike of London returned to her. Varlissima was too kind to remind Allison that England was in the middle of the Atlantic Ocean, so fog there was to be expected.

In any case, they kept this distant relationship for several years with Allison and Tony. It was polite, and distant, and possibly misinformed by the rumor mills. Then, suddenly, George and Varlissima were invited over to dinner.

This was early in the spring of 2040, a time of alarm.

Evidence Is the Meal

The meal was meticulous; Allison talked about her representation of the great eccentrics of her agency, some capable of making the early writer Thomas Pynchon look logical. Salman Rushdie was declared a pure "purse" genius, "long life to him." She struck at memories with the tang of strange fruit. When it came to these writers, she was at home.

George's first thought, often overexcited and misinformed, was that Allison's breathiness might be the result of a traumatic brain injury.

Allision was an immediate success to George and Varlissima, since her verbal acuity lifted all veils dramatically. While her husband Tony had no visible first principles, and seemed a deep proponent of the state of things, she said that she had once visited Leningrad before the pandemic.

This was a telling tale. She had been given a map of Leningrad by her husband, who normally was always by her side whenever she ventured outside, anywhere. But that day she wanted us to know that she went out on her own for a few hours. You could feel the mounting corrections about to burst from Tony on her tale.

She got lost in following a bird around a corner. She could see several grand Russian orthodox churches before her. Vivid.

Yet there was no trace of them on Tony's Russian-made map.

No trace, not even an icon. Tony had failed to tell Allison that the Russians "after their great change"—as he referred to it—decided to not show churches on their modern maps!

She did see one orientating church on the map, however, which, thank God, helped her find her way back to the hotel, heart in hand, and eyes as wide as a bullet train's front lights.

Tony reminded her, when she arrived rattled and safe, "Dear, how silly of you. They showed that church that saved you from yourself because it is a museum. They only show living churches, museums, and call all the rest dead."

As if that detail mattered.

Tony was a rarified electrical engineer—a man who lived a life of heroic detail rather than emotion—who worked for one of the Technology Ministry's manufacturers of the most advanced silicon wafers, "which made the toys of Intel look childish," he would say. It was easy to feel an undifferentiated rage at Tony; the way George felt about his mechanic when the Lexus repair bill was four times what he thought necessary or possible. There was a technological arrogance about the man that ran supreme.

When you asked what he meant by "childish," he shed a look of "I am sorry, but I cannot say more." He had us wrapped around his fingers, as the things in the room spoke for him. Tony was a man of things; militant in his silence, and certain in his views. He knew more about machines than children, so the comparison was false.

Tony had a room full of the tools of known special ops forces. He let you handle the foldable SATCOM communications antenna—its black shine had a feel of fine finish on wood—and the electronic handset for secure communications with a virtually limitless range. These looked like the things of his life. When asked, Tony did not say much about how he came across them.

They were all kept in mint condition, Marine style plus.

Tony and His Machines

Over the years, George, capable of informed paranoia, told his wife that Tony had invented key parts of facial recognition and AI in the 2020s. By 2040, this mattered increasingly to George.

There was no formal evidence for this claim.

Half of this internal narrative about AI and facial recognition was in the storage channels of George's self-informing mind. "Sure, we see what we expect," he told Varlissima, "however, look around his rooms. They speak volumes."

George based his thesis on one thing Tony had said once, outside, on a frigid early spring morning, getting his mail, that seared a hole in George's mind: "What I do matters. The discovery of surplus memory enables our machines to predict personalization. I have invented and amended the machines that sort through all patterns of behavior."

George remembered Tony going on, when Tony noted:

"You can no longer camouflage inner wars of the self because you have accumulated definitive clicks over time. It does not matter what psychodrama exists in a person anymore. What matters is their aggregated service to the state. Our machines of the State can now repattern the horrors of self-doubt that have plagued humanity from its start—and we offer solutions. This is our gift to humanity. Let them now eat hamburgers in peace and prosperity, and throw out the sins of misperception."

Tony's praise of these devices had an ancient and a modern feel to them. The machinery of memory, always an object of control by those making myths, were in the hands of technical elites now. You had to wonder how— and when—Tony would bring these gadgets even further into our futures.

Surplus Memory and The Neighborhood

Native humanists, living in a rural past, believed in the *Natura*, or natural halo, of a person. There is a general historic belief that one human can understand the essence of another person, without many words, even across cultures and languages. In addition, these humanists gave society the confidences that once you began in an exchange, a dialogue, with different parties, a shared understandable feeling of community could be achieved—that a feeling of being human was achievable in groups. This feeling, almost magical to anthropologists, was deeper, and more mysterious, than family clans or even tribes. It was the pulse of humanity itself, like the pattern of the sun each morning.

Machines made all of these beliefs idle and dream-like.

Surplus memory was one of those magical focus phrases that contained all of 2040 in a single phrase. It was both a TV jingle and a total jungle. It was exacting, too. And it lacked what George called "literary ambiguity." George, like many idle humanists, could afford to celebrate literary ambiguity. He had once noted in his journals that there are 7.5 types of ambiguity, with a smile and a tilt in his hat that morning to William Empson. Yet Tony would view such things as childish.

"Surplus memory" suggested both a gift and a robbery; both a positive and a negative gift. It was both winter and summer, both fall and spring. It contained how the State wanted to control human imagination.

You can agree, between neighbors, whether a bird is a greater-in-size gull than usual. You sit there and watch, and as the bird slowly circles round and hovers with its outstretched wings, the observer can calculate the true dimensions of the bird and deduce, despite all of the birds, trembling, its size.

Yet when it comes to the human spirit, and our memory, our very *Natura*, as George's grandmother trained him to attend to—such calculations have evaded the State for centuries. You cannot really tell size or impact. Humanists are people who need to become over time; any snapshot is inaccurate. They become themselves in a fashion both lovely and deeper than any accumulated data snapshot. Tony suggested he could now, however, map a person's nature definitively. This proved, for George, Abe, and Varlissima, menacing.

And after that, Tony was probably recruited for more invisible work, George suspected, where he might have spent decades advancing for the Eight Nation States' voice recognition systems.

Tony was a warrior, no doubt about that. He must have moved rapidly from visual to aural surveillance. They called it "psycho-crafting devices." The things Tony brought into our neighborhood assured us that we were not off the beaten path, but instead, that our concerns and movements were being well monitored.

The Roman Calendar

April Fools' Day was nearing, a ritualized time of celebration and relaxation after the long winter. The presence of Tony continued to annoy. Even Abe got agitated sometimes, reflecting on what Tony might be up to. The suspicion in the neighborhood grew. Was it envy at all his fancy machines? Was it suspicion derived from the way he seemed to control Allison?

Tony noted, once, while entering his spotless truck to catch a quick bite of ice cream downtown, that it was "the discovery of memory surplus that enables us to better fit people to the public."

This suggested that there was, in fact, in the market, maybe even available at Walmart or Build Back Better Best Buy, some social engineering tools Tony had modified for popular use, like night vision and optics. Besides electronics, some of the early versions of statecraft equipment were made public.

George was convinced that Tony had all this in his past. Abe, a dear friend, warned: "Yes, George, but what is the value of such speculation? What matters is what happens today and tomorrow. Better to file the paper stories, and get on with it. We can conquer tomorrow today if we pay attention to what is before us in the news, not what is merely in the past of our neighbors." It was a haunting and generous suggestion.

Without a doubt, George felt Tony was a leader, a chief, within the State's "Search Teams." George had heard about this elite group of high-tech folks. They take the electronic daily scroll of global news, pattern it, and instantly feed it back to the Event Police on the streets, copied by elaborate lists and trails to the State officials themselves. These were the aggregated gold nuggets whereby people became more and more isolated in their neighborhoods. They were already themselves, defined and patterned, before they became fully themselves.

Early one morning George believed he saw, near 4:15 a.m., a silver reflective hovercraft lift Tony up to work. It was almost indiscernible in the dark, and hardly made a hum in the trees.

George called Tony's latest system "astral listening." George suggested again to Varlissima and Abe that the Big Eight Nations could hear foreign and domestic conversations from a thousand miles away. Varlissima responded: "George, you know you are losing your hearing. Stop all that masculine fantasizing." Abe agreed. Another week passed on Stone Church Road. The way she pronounced "fantasizing" had a real zing to it. He loved being scolded by his wife.

April Fools

There is something about April 1 that makes even an old writer feel feisty. The popular embrace of a day of joking brought joy to George. "We all begin to listen to the astral whispering of the trees, the shrill departure of winter, the beginning of our spiritual thawing, even if we are pagans and thieves"—noted the ever-cynical Winston. April 1 is our fools' day; a day of joy, of opening, of saying: "Let's stay all day outside"—for the first time in what seems like years.

And like most men approaching that forever-receding hairline of older age, George made each story about Tony bigger with time.

Across the last three Aprils, the pattern of storytelling about Tony's past increased in its pressure and purposes for George. It grew in George's mind like a headache. At its peak, some afternoons, George's thought of one of Tony's machines caused a physical twinge in his back.

George, in his replays, added words to the twists and the turns of Tony. He used Tony as some kind of ancient leveling force, like the ones used by the general leveling commission in France—the NGF—that placed lovely metal markers under porches and beside walls as height indicators in case of flood. George was out to tell the neighborhood what he saw. It was as simple as that; yet the actual act of telling them something that mattered was in question.

George wanted to be observant and to be accurate, like an ancient chronicler of human nature itself. He wanted to measure the dangers and daring of Tony without a word to any, except Varlissima and his collage mate

Abe. There were plenty of words to attach to an evil spirit without needing to take it as public as a Puritan. As we age, especially during April Fools' Day, we can afford the time to take the measure of our neighbors, and we do.

Total Awareness

Since 2020, it was known by many that self-authorized extracts of our memories into machines gave the Big Eight—that State—special new controls. The State was the Big Eight and the Big Eight was the State.

This was true for every season, every day, of the years we used our computers or handhelds. The companies called it "Total Awareness Profiling," something matured first by global firms like GE under the 360° interviewing process. But now it had become purely quantitative, based on sensors and a few Event Police, not interviews. The State had profiles on all of us, without needing to meet many of us.

These memory machines gave the State unprecedented skills at measuring obedience in the populace, by evaluating their buying habits from their computer purchases, and by observing them "in the net," a synthesis of their behaviors before the Event Police. Each neighbor had a number—an elevation number—that helped the State keep tally.

A set of well-paid Harvard researchers, funded by the Department of Defense across the Alliance, had established this as real and functional. A few European courts had taken the companies to task for their deliberate invasions of privacy. Nonetheless, the Big Eight nations, in gentle defiance of the overconcerned Europeans, instituted surplus memory AI in every urban area of the world. It only took 15 years, from 2025 to 2040, for most mega-cities to achieve alignment with these policy goals.

This went well beyond the profits of Facebook, Google, and Apple. This was State-sponsored work. George was beginning to suspect that it was Tony's primary job to bring these new monitoring devices into the neighborhood of Stone Church Road.

Love of State

This entire mapping of neighborhoods by the State went underground. By 2040, much was covered on TV, Twitter, or in the print press regarding The Big Eight Nations, but not a single screen on any given neighborhood. Those were covered within each Facetime neighborhood nexus.

These forms of electronic control did not need laws, or rules, or disclosure to blossom each season. George feared that somehow Tony would detect his suspicions. There was some paranoia in most neighborhoods about these advances, but most did not know what to do about it. The march of these machines continued daily into the last few decades, untouched by journalists and thought leaders.

George loved his family more than The Big Eight. Perhaps he was myopic, but he loved his neighborhood, and its grand trees, the small stone church, more than most global things. "Allison can love her classics, and Varlissima can love her birds. We need to be alert to these machines spying on our cares."

Few worried even half as much as George. "George is a worry bug," Varlissima said to the neighbors.

The State of Play

The Stone Church neighborhood was not authorized to know how the updates of surplus memory were occurring, as an agreement between the elected Mayors kept peace near K Creek. While it was still humanly possible to guess about the nature of a neighbor—we still had the emotive genes for all that—it was not possible to monitor or to measure the progress of machines.

Tony and Allison, as a childless couple, had the time to establish a higher order to their worries. This was a feature of the technical elite. For others, the most important relationships within our family were those between parents and their children. For Tony, the State seemed to loom even larger than family, having zero knowledge of the intimacy of a daughter to a father.

George worried about this. Could one really understand human needs if they lacked a deep connection to children and their future? If he ran the hiring practices of the Big Eight monitoring teams, he would never give a prominent job to a childless engineer.

Measured and Monitored

George felt he and Varlissima were being measured, monitored, but he did not know exactly why. That is what annoyed the shit out of Abe, and what gave George pause.

Even if you strained your eyes with a magnifier glass to read the fine print that came with any of your electronic devices and hand-computers, it was damn difficult to tell what was yours and what was theirs. The entire universe seemed to stream through these devices. You were given the feeling that somehow you had the right to all of it. Yet George felt he knew better.

In other words, we were measured and monitored but did not have a firm sense of where we stood. In the old days, in the days of print media for the first 400 years, towns like Saratoga were quite stable. From a Ben Franklin pamphlet to a college degree, things in print lasted. Towns were towns, political favors were common and noticeable, and neighborhoods discrete and crisp. You could hang them up, share them, make sense of them, debate them. Neighborhoods were more open. But today, in the month of

April, our lives are a moving target. This evaluation of our elevation was the new State-sponsored game.

Over the last three, long years, Tony, in George's mind, invented most of the things in the general realm of surveillance. Machine intelligence was as different from print media as an automobile was from a horse.

Again, all of this concern might only be in George's head. Varlissima reminded her husband that the problem with paranoia is that even if you were right you were wrong; and she restated that that was true in Italy during Mussolini, and in Germany during Hitler, and that it seemed always true. "Better not to worry too much, George. We are safe."

Dinner with Tony

It is now April 20, Earth Day across the Big Eight Nations.

George and Varlissima sat amazed at this first dinner with Allison and Tony. The place is meticulous, everything in place. The stone fireplace made Varlissima's 19th-century stone fireplace appear exceedingly dirty. Each leather-bound book looks in sequence, as if they read not only with passion but also with a tight-fisted discipline.

The works of George Orwell are prominent. You see the latter-day apocalyptic writers of the last few decades, such as Bill McKibben, who have been calling for the end of the world for fifty years. Strange that such an orderly couple would want to study this apocalypse.

It is a smart home—music joins you as you walk between rooms. Each electronic recording of Bach, Beethoven, Brahms, and the other German imperialists plays in alphabetical order. There is not a single pile of anything, anywhere. Meticulous, over-groomed, like 10 Downing Street. George explained that some of this music technology had been installed by 2025 by Applied Materials in the Museum of Rock and Roll. Tony displayed the purchased yellow tags on each perched piece of the equipment, like a badge of courage. These were not inexpensive toys.

In a house of such technological splendor, George pondered the constant flow of information pouring out of the house and into the couple. "This tyranny of endless recorded actions and opinion spouts in this house indicate mind control," he thought. Why did Tony and Allison need so much order in their lives? Why did they not simply enjoy the disorder of Bob Dylan's mind? Dylan offered them a cheaper, more entertaining, more diverse path into the modern times, without a need for all the surveillance equipment.

Varlissima remained fascinated by the colorful design and interior grandeur of the things themselves. The place was a museum of the modern. Without any doubt, Allison was superior in interior decoration. Tony excelled in his sense of control.

The Family Parrot

Tony had a brightly colored, greenish-yellow Latin American parrot. Allison alerted them to the fact that the bird "was like John Steinbeck's *The Red Pony*, but better." Tony brought the parrot with them to the dozen places they lived. The parrot was addressed formally as "Sir William." He looked heavy as a chicken, but poised in a strange, almost human stare from the cage. Allison said, "When Sir William came into my life, I was not ready, at first, for his hot-tempered ways. But as Sir William got older, and had a few bouts of illness in our home, he taught me more clearly about the ways of nature and the ways of man."

George recorded in his mind: "The dinner starts perfectly normal. Nothing in particular worth remembering. Except for this odd, green bird, Sir William."

They chatted about the last cleanup weekend the spring before; how the Russian immigrants down the road were "actually nice." Tony reminded us that the Tower of Babel fell "when the workforce no longer would understand each other." As if workflow and words were the only ways to define human competence.

That felt like a divine weapon and a lead balloon dropped swiftly into conversation. Sir William even pivoted his head at that comment.

They moved on, chatting about neighbors. Allison brought up the excess of immigrants down the road. There were these submerged themes of hatred against all immigrants in Tony and Allison; a mainstreaming in their memories from all their travels, a kind of disrobing of racial or tribal differences. Very strange. Very strange, indeed.

They got up from the table.

In the new room George eyed the dive knives and snorkels. Allison saw the overt assault zone markers they would put down on the roadside so no one would get hit while doing the debris pickup.

They got to talking again about Tony's work—which, again, remained mysterious. Then they slipped, inadvertently, into Politics. Wamp. What a turn of events.

It turns out that both Tony and Allison were conspiratorialists.

They were power elites of the Eight Nations. Their friends all went to the same schools since youth. They didn't really care about the common man; instead, they felt that any day soon "the gentle, well-equipped people" would launch a revolution. Tony and Allison had their gear ready in the basement, asking George and Varlissima if they wanted to see it another time.

At first Varlissima thought they are kidding. It would have been a sportive finale to a wonderful evening. In an act of silent discretion, George pressed her inner thigh under the table. She offered a yelp.

They proceeded with the dinner.

They touch on public matters like community, a sense of the neighborhood, matters of our own identity—but never a thing about Tony. And George felt more than ever that Tony was keeping Allison stable, keeping her on a lease of sanity she did not really want.

The dessert was as good.

It was as sweet and healthy as they get, all in one, a combination of home-made vanilla ice cream, soft Austrian cake with just the right lift, and some "life of chocolate flakes" to boot.

They smiled, left, and hopped across the road, back home at last. They felt violated but did not fully know why.

The Morning After

The next morning Varlissima had an idea. They had to return to complete the feeling, to make the bond seal.

She was by nature a generous soul. This clashed as the opposite of Tony's secretive nature. Tony was about grand things like ancestor worship, divine weapons, supreme military beings, sacred sites in war, and how a singular human should never forget their accomplishments.

Varlissima was all about care, about relationships, about differences. George felt she was always editing other people's carefully crafted words on a page so they looked better. She was about our neighborhood, not the State at large, its natural splendor, the change of seasons, the flow of the creek and the flight of the birds. Varlissima was capable of recalling so much detail about being outside each day: the passing of what bird and when, or the babies being born in the bird boxes she had placed herself throughout the neighborhood. She was the opposite of Tony's modern machinery.

George said they were oil and water. In rather mythic and anthropological terms, George's daily journal was full of noted differences.

The next morning, Varlissima and George were being visited, by chance, for the day, by their daughter Colette, a doctor and a darling. Varlissima and Colette, feeling obliged to return some favors from the stunning dinner the night before, walked back over to Tony and Allison, this time with a small gift. For women like Varlissima, there was nothing more sacred than a gift from a daughter that involved fertility rights and nature itself.

The gift was a small drawing Colette had made of a fox standing up near an abandoned tripod camera in the woods.

Bob Dylan had put his subjects on chrome horses, and in awkward angles. This drawing by Colette was pure and simple, and the only artificial thing in the entire scene was the camera. Her rendering of the camera was not as sexy as the polished black and yellow Gentex Jump-Helmet we saw in Tony's photo shop, which had a free-fall parachute jump tied on it. Colette's gift was still by a fine neighborhood artist and heartfelt. In contrast, Colette's rendering had warmth in it, and the fox's posture delighted.

She did this drawing in pure fancy, nothing more, nothing less. This in itself had the power of a nobler type of humanity. A gift from a young artist suspends time; it remains an intention for the future. It occupies a space of care.

On top of that, Varlissima thought Tony would get a kick out of this gift, since he had expensive photographic equipment, and they both had showed their amazing film development laboratory in their former bathroom.

Standing at the door, after Varlissima and Colette presented the gift, Tony took it and placed it prematurely under his arm. Without a word, he processed the gift.

He then brought them both before Allison, inside the alcove of the home. To revisit their things—the parrot, the lovely porch, the devices, and the silence of about what Tony really did.

When Varlissima came back home, she used the word "stern" to describe their neighbors. George asked, "Did Colette say something wrong?"

"No," noted Varlissima. "Perhaps Tony noticed my yelp at the dinner, and concluded something conspiratorial about it."

The next week Tony took a "bigger job" in Maine; where they moved with great precision in exactly three days.

Chapter Three:
The Poles Resist the Dream Book

There was more room for wandering in the mind now that Tony had left town. For now, April 30, the neighborhood felt larger, more inclusive, magical. It was getting closer to game time.

This home, this neighborhood, is Abe and Winston, Winston and Abe.

His friends knew what was next. April 30 happens to be a sacred time as well—the birthday of Varlissima. They knew enough to put their hands high toward the ceiling, well above their heads, bowing on entry to the birthday girl.

We wake up each morning with the bright illusion of choice before us. We feel we can meet anyone, do anything, when in reality joy resides in finding the right mix of friends, knowing the blueprints of their soul, and enjoying them with some abandon and trust. We do not get around as much as we once did before the Virus.

This bonding is the stuff of friendship, and the only way to survive this damn pandemic.

It was edging the burst of full spring in the neighborhood. Dutch bulbs were beginning to pop their green heads out of the soil, ready to be turned yellow if a frost happened after Mother's Day, as it had several times during his stay near the Church.

The leaves of the vast variety of trees were budding, tuning themselves with the longer sun. George noticed things, like how the sunflower leaves daily aligned with the path of the sun. New bird sounds started to arrive—the robins' company meant much, as they scanned the lawn for worms. Abe suggested that the "return of spring allows ethical thought."

Overall, as friends, we had defeated the anxieties of youth and survived the family obligations of middle age. We were now in this long, ruminating platform known as our elder years.

When spring arrived, we could stand tall. Full of sound and the visual, the K Creek broke up its frozen face for us. The breeding season came fast all around us. Time for new thoughts in old bodies.

The first banners of spring read, hanging from the Church:

Isolation of the self creates alarm and the fear

Goodbye winter, hello katydids, birds, and blooms.

Friends are extremely important in 2040, for there is enough piety and danger in any neighborhood to fill a lifetime with worry and concerns of no consequence. There are many people who do not have the freedoms to notice the birds and the bees, and are instead, made by machines, locked in a fierce hatred.

You can consume a life noticing with rage new entries per second on Twitter, and waste another late night or morning on the stupa, the gates, to nowhere.

The machines that accompany spring never stop.

They hum in your pockets, on your desk, in your car, until they are part of your temple. You get nowhere without them. Spring arrives—you are still locked in an endless, seasonless year of tweets. Friendships allow one to climb past the hum of these machines and to kiss the top of someone's best thoughts, and still be yourself. Friends were extremely important to 2040.

Song to Friendship

Friends can help save high-maintenance people, like George, from themselves; and they can help stop the storms of self-doubt in its tracks. This trio were mentors to each other, fathers to their future selves.

The bird song shared by these three friends increased its raucousness each new Spring. They knew they would not live forever as a trio, so why pretend? They were not ridiculous, like those making riddles of everyday. They were raucous in their thoughts, like friends. When you had time on your hands, and were recording your remaining days, three friends provided a trinity of possibilities.

George's greatest accomplishment in life was bringing his college mates to the neighborhood. Over the years, they had come to like Colette and Varlissima. This helped the self-absorbed aspects of each of the three of them get tempered by the good charm of smart women.

George had encouraged their moves across years and months. He was ready to confess he manipulated these friends, so that they were near him. He spent years, while they were in Manhattan and Philadelphia, working on them. He never shared the dread of a Saratoga winter with them! Instead, he involved them in the march of months toward glorious race track season, and then through the glories of fall.

By exposing them to Saratoga at the right times of year, well before the chill of February, they sold their city homes, took the killings, and came into paradise near the Creek. George called this his "tribute to friendship."

The New Bird Songs

Each day since college George aroused into life—some morns into a kind of hyper-alertness—by conversations with these friends.

Winston and Abe.

Abe and Winston.

Like fine insects wiggling in the sky. George had several dozen good friends, but Abe and Winston were particularly keen friends. They landed near him; knowing life short, in his head, they began to screech.

They grew with each other; learning as they went. They felt for each other; sparing no thoughts from each other. They were friends for life. They'd laugh, and cry. They'd do everything but sleep on each other's shoulders. But most often, they loved watching sports together.

Each morning George heard echoes of the prior day's conversations—the abstract studied neutrality of Winston; the detailed, daily passions of Abe, the man of the hour, the man of the news, the man with his eyes wide open.

"I would have remained a factory kid and a basketball star were it not for Abe and Winston," George announced this spring.

Watching Games

While the three of them had traveled large portions of the world for work and pleasure before the pandemic, they stuck close at home in the Stone Church neighborhood after the widespread disease and the series of storms of late. This got them more intimately involved in basketball games on four-dimensional television sound dynamics, where you could spin with the players. They surprised themselves with their talent for watching games.

For by 2040, when you were rich, like each of them, you can avoid contagion as you isolate, and continue having fun. Abe reminded them, on occasion, "There is a cruelty in this distance." But they did not let it deeply disturb them.

They could afford the best vicarious seats at the end of seasons; and they did not miss whatever was available. This allowed them to watch basketball even during the time of mosquitoes. Spring wildflowers were vivid now on the nature trails by their homes.

May was the month.

May was marvelous.

"Goodnight, moon," they'd remember to say as the games ended.

The next morning George recalled the conversations, saying in his journal: "You could indulge in the vast universe of consumer goods, and not think. Our story is different, concerning the digs and jabs and jives between these friends. Being well-educated, and argumentative by nature, we remain alert to the world's issues." George sincerely believed they were not lost in the arrogant daze of idle wealth. Instead, they lifted their days out of obscurity through the scrutiny of themselves.

As friends, they had shared a great deal together.

They had been to Sicily, on three separate occasions; once for the Norman churches, once for the pure tour of the regional and excellent food, and the last time for the rural towns—where they looked for African, Italian, and continental influences in architecture and foods. Now they were stuck home for three years in a row, 2037 to 2040.

Stuck at Home

Winston was their resident expert on all things involving politics, the State, the Eight Nations, reunification, loyalties, factions, resentments, and tactics.

Abe was the resident expert on all things dealing with individual news stories of the day and region, with a special and witty ability to bring the outside world into their day-to-day reporting and discussions. It was like a 24/7 news team, in a sense, but deeper and more informed because these friends were friends, in and out.

When George spoke about basketball, he spoke with authority, explaining himself as a man in full bloom. When he spoke about other things—such as politics or the weather—he showed himself to have profound differences from Winston, and less so from Abe. Yet because they knew each other for decades, they were passionate and amiable about most subjects and most experiences. This gave a delight to their buzz.

It was better than television, these conversations, as they became the substance in life as they aged on Stone Church Road. As the seasons proceeded with rapid play, professional basketball grew into a global passion. Players of skill arrived from each corner of the world, tall, slender, and fantastic. The great teams, like the 2035 Spurs and the 2038 Rockets, the Lakers and the Celtics, were perfect in range and mix of cultures. It was a global sport with magnificent athletes.

They had grace and force, and proved so fascinating that the everyday bigot forgot about race, and admired "these exceptional players." It helped them hit play, not pause, in their lives. Never a negative from Allison about these b-ball players.

The Poles, Oh the Poles

Great light and joy approaches in the middle of May.

The subtle but stable joys in a Mother's Day. Black flies are being born, billions of them, in jest and earnest.

The neighbors are rushing around, planting new shrubs and flowers before those bastard flies arrive from up in the Adirondacks. It has been a noble race in Saratoga most Mays.

George and Varlissima plant their new ones late into the dusk, as a few early-season fireflies greet them in their yard over from the neighbor's pond. Life is good in May, as the days end.

Thinking of what his ancestors did on their farm in Poland, George noticed the pattern of the bats before game time. They came into his flight path each night, gliding about 20 to 50 feet above his head. When the insects were abundant—*zum zap sum fly*—so were the bats arriving each night from behind the church in droves. The bats made a Lockheed Martin Mach 4 fighter jet look obsolete in their rapid success at the bugs each night. Varlissima noticed that some of the bats emerge at dusk from behind the church front door, wedging their fates between the stone and the doorframe.

During the last three years of isolation, George developed a deeper addiction to his favorite basketball team, the Poles. He liked everything about them.

Their mascot was an excited dog. In the icon of this black wiggling dog, the electronic experts had embedded a device where its fluffy tail was in a constant, endless wag. The mascot himself seemed animated, eager to prove that the Poles had an interest in their audience. This dog was a god of dogs, you might say. In a world where many things fought for their attention, George found this team and this dog loveable.

The Poles were the best at being down-to-earth. "A Day in the Life of the Poles," a weekly show on 4DTV, found the players shopping in supermarkets for a range of spicy, fresh sausages. The Poles exercised with hand radios near, as they sliced onions for their horseradish without tearing up. They were always hungry to win. They made each other look good on the court. The court was their domain. Compared to many athletic stars in 2040, the Poles were the working-class team. Coming from Polish decent, George was proud, fundamentally, of the Poles.

Watching them, George escaped. Born into poverty, fatherless, it was odd to find himself wealthy in this neighborhood. Watching the Poles reminded him of his native competitiveness that allowed his ascent. Yet watching them, he also remembered his origins.

He had been put on the mask of anti-depressants once or twice during stressful times. These days seemed distant now, like a forgotten plot in a late evening film. He found when he indulged in writing and in basketball, he could get off the numbing stuff. How exciting to realize that big pharma could be made obsolete by the simple fog machines of a good game and a sheet of paper.

Rancid seasons, rotten egg days had passed in his life; but when watching men and women drive baseline, he felt life. While watching a basketball game, George entered a null set in his skull. The speed of the passing, the relentlessness of the competition—these mattered. It all mattered. Again and again and again, game after game after game. He achieved total relaxation from the State during game time, a rare set of moments in a world where devices ring almost every ten minutes. This fixation with the Poles helped. The Poles were completely old-world. "A pure play," Abe would say, noting George a simple man, a good man.

George, a person who preferred isolation, did like company when he watched a game. George was beaming, happy that his two friends were often there with him.

Wait, his mind went into pause.

Wait, he said to himself. Wait....

* * * * *

Ok, I will now admit it.

I am George.

I am writing about my neighborhood.

My life.

My friends.

I really do not know why I did not confess this before. Why did I hide behind that literary veil, this convention, until now?

Was I afraid of rejection? Was it that I was afraid you would discount my tale? Was it that I'd rather have you know Tony and Allison, Abe and Winston, than myself? No simple direct answer jumped to the page. Perhaps indirection was simpler.

I do have a sense of humor. Perhaps it was because these characters made me do it! They were more interesting, more meaningful, more hilarious than I. To pivot like this requires your sense of humor, now, too.

This sportive seriousness helps me survive trauma, such as when my father died before me. I can see the hallway between the bathroom and his bedroom, but I cannot see him.

I was three when Walt died. I cannot see him bleeding, but I feel the blood inside my head, even at 75. I can feel it pulsing. No one can ever fully understand this about me. I grew up in a neighborhood of factory workers. In my early days competing on the street, most felt me an immigrant, and called me so. Today we'd think of my neighborhood of origin as a prosperous slum. You had enough to eat, but no medical insurance, few cars. I could have given up before I began.

But I am no couch potato.

My Puerto Rican brothers were small potatoes. White society was sternly biased against their lives, making them shrink with time. They did not bud early like me, being Caucasian; teachers shortchanged Edwin and Theo, offering them no mentoring. My brothers married early, at sixteen and seventeen, before a full education, and split for Puerto Rico, leaving the mainland and thus freed into their own narrowing lives. Then again, I got schooling because I could shoot the long ball.

My mother was a sweet potato.

My Chinese American sister, Susie Jing Chang, became an adopted potato, and was mixed into a rich elite California family, becoming the family's new exotic flower. Susie was loved deeply by me and my biological sister; but she is now a missing person in our lives.

My uncles, who were janitors and landscapers, were proud men and kind immigrants who over time became mashed potatoes. They taught me how to keep competitive and masculine in my pride, being fatherless. Yet while my basketball skills got me to college, they remained laborers until they died early. This all seems like fiction now. When I started ascending in White society, few had reason to look into my mixed background.

Leaving the First Home

There is a kind of self-delusion that trips you up if you escaped your first prisons in youth. A home in poverty has small walls and a ceiling you can touch in the morning. You begin to assume greater things are possible. It takes persistence to slip out of all-encompassing captivity. All lives are captive in their options; but when one is born poor and smart, that is a particular prison. Yet when you escape you then face a bigger box.

My college professors did not know how to size me up; and they filled my brain with exemplars well beyond my need and reach. Walt Whitman. Ralph Waldo Emerson, the Norton Anthologies. You did not have time to think through to the future, when you were so much in the grand and eloquent past. I had already graduated several survival tests from ten to seventeen. Ivy League college seemed like a paid vacation. Yet it has taken me decades to realize how they simply put me in another box, a box of the third person, indirection and civility.

Without disclosure, there is only disaster. Without self-reflection, there is only self-delusion. As my grandmother stated in a mantra worth repeating: "Truth decays like tooth decay."

I am simply George.

Why I Wore a Noh Mask

We wear masks for infection now. Yet being a businessman, when home or abroad, is like wearing a mask.

In Noh theatre, the true genuine face of the actor is kept hidden—as they are not people but universal types. The face of rage. The face of fear. The face of beauty. I was the face of competition—raw, unadulterated competition. It was all about winning the game of earning. Nothing personal. Nothing expressive. While my life was bizarre, I still kept the mask tight on my face. Until now.

Whenever I wrote in the third person, I felt like a ladybug born in late October, trying to get through the small seams of doorframes, into the warmth of someone else's home. I knew it was cold outside. I was accustomed to this feeling of needing to escape. It had been that way for me since I was three. But I was never really home, I was lost in the tradition.

The third-person persona provided a strange wrinkle in time, a protective plastic way to hide the friendly arteries really beating in my heart. No one that paid me knew the true George, they knew the reliability of the masks. I worked for over a hundred companies with a Noh mask on; it worked.

When freed of masks, we can invent endless things to talk about if you give me the chance. Even shopping in a supermarket can be illuminating.

Going to the movies, sitting on my ass, talking to the universe. The entire universe becomes Whitmanesque, intriguing, worth reflection and capture.

"For you, George, Mr. Life Force, it proves the only way to find grace and enjoyment in the divine isolation of today," noted the brilliant Abe. Winston did not give a shit about my origins.

I know today that part of my mask was built while I was going to elite schools. They were designed to make me repressed, civilized, more Noh. They designed my memories, as they do for thousands each semester.

I was graded, at times, on my behavior and appearance more than my substance or my defiance. And defiance was always filed at, like fingernails grown too long. "Be Cornell," a few of the professors said, mostly men back then, "And this means dignified." I loved my professors, but deep down, the years on the street made me realize they were fools, in a tower of elite, reconfirming but repressive echoes.

These elites do not rule the world, they push papers about the world. "Think about it," I said to Abe and Winston on several occasions. They did not listen, growing impatient.

Writing in the third person is like working your whole life for the Global Bureau of Investigations. In fact, look who populates those buildings: kids from the best prep schools and the elite universities. Although invited into the corridors of power, you began to think crooked. "You do not know the needs of the people," notes Abe. "You do not know the world," notes Varlissima. You forget how huge the sunflowers are in your own yard, as you serve the State in crystal cities, with large computer screens before you, monitoring the growing unrest. Winston never admitted this as we chatted on such subjects as a quartet. He chose silence on the subject of elite education's downward twirl and hidden repression.

Since Chaucer, the tradition of the third person serves as a kind of fog. Have you enjoyed any of the contemporary translations of *The Canterbury Tales*? Did you ask, "Who the hell is that third person after all? Who is Chaucer's baker, really? The priest? That beautiful Italian girl who marries the Middle Eastern ruler, and then comes back to Rome? Who is she? Even worse, who is this great and only Chaucer?"

Many of these great books of the past are all in the third person, deeply hidden, however revealing. We do not get the lurid first person of Walt Whitman until 1855, and that, too, took more than a hundred years to take root.

We have more immediacy in the modern.

Whenever I brought this need for differentiation of the self for immediacy to Abe, he said, "I get it." Whenever I brought the same up to Winston, he'd say, "Wait a minute, George, the stifling humidity and heat of ego-based reporting is suspect. The State wants to note patterns, buying patterns, not thoughts. Your individual observations, your specific thoughts, count for shit."

Oh, the delight in being able to use the weight of real words to navigate between Winston and Abe, between Abe and Winston.

Only the imagination—and diverse reading—is free to do this. "Just my type," Varlissima had once said about me, as we shared an early meal before marriage eons ago. We talked books, took long free walks, rode bicycles—leaving the assumptions of State ascent behind. We were back-to-the-earthers before Earth was taken hostage by the State.

When you start writing about yourself—about the stunning romance of the self, like my man Walt Whitman did—that is when your dreams release into lived experience, when the sky is the limit. Bullets fly around corners. You are out on the street, walking with friends in the great parks, and no longer stuck in the cells of the Global Bureau of Investigations.

You are living.

The Rumors Began

It took us some time to drive down to the game, but it was worth it—Winston, Abe, and myself have supreme tickets. We are at a game, thank the gods for that.

Before the game starts, I do need to react to an annoying feature in our lives. As soon as we began our drive to the Pepsi Arena, there was a rumor in the neighborhood that began to fly. I chose to ignore the handheld alerts as the scandal escalated.

The Event Police suggested that Allison's niece had shared secrets and bad blood about the actual ways Allison's adoptive mother reshaped her personality while still in London.

Our electronic devices can do this until we go lunatic: always suggesting some outlaw thing is happening in a relatively stable society, where the rich get richer as all others fight about things they cannot have. It is cruel, really. Yet so many find it consuming and entertaining.

It happens often when you leave your neighborhood. When you leave a town, you find you have a slippery social status. And as you get further from your neighborhood, there are suggestions that you are in debt, or you are secretly short of cash, or you befriended too many Russians, or you have a stipend that you lost meant for your daughter's education. It is all silly and annoying, yet it works for most that remain in the neighborhood.

This is how the State keeps you in the neighborhood; as you notice the pattern, as you leave, each mile, your elevation numbers drop.

These automatic news updates, on their binging, black hand-held devices, claimed Allison's mother was cruel and undereducated, compared to Allison. Big shit, I thought. Yet it amused my companions.

Apparently, Allison earned a doctoral degree before coming to Saratoga. Excerpts were shared from it, where she examined, through case work, the qualities women embody that enable male predators to select and to focus on them. The shrinks labeled this phenomenon "the attractant personality." This theme caused her British stepmother much embarrassment in her neighborhood back in England, as if wanting to study this subject was itself somehow suggesting something shamefully wrong about her adopted daughter. Silly, but true in the U.K.

There were many pictures sent to us of her mother retreating from Allison's kiss.

These stupid alerts noted that Allison took psychology courses at Adelphi University on Long Island, during her days as a Manhattan agent, to make sense of her troubled life. Again, I found these comments from the State fickle and outrageous instances of bad faith. Yet they kept streaming.

I would rather watch basketball deep into the night, and read classics, then stoop to such constant belittling annoyances. Although always fascinated with any revelations of family trauma, I steered clear of listening intently to Abe reading out these alerts as we drove to Albany. Abe, being a journalist, cannot get enough updates per hour as we drove to the game

The game was far more revealing in potential to me than anything in the news, so I ignored the hourly updates from the neighborhood. Winston and Abe remained riveted, having left the intrigues of our neighborhood in body only.

Game Time at Pepsi Arena

We arrived happy at the site of the game in Albany's arena near 5:00 P.M. The boys put down their devices, at last. I even asked if I could lock them in the glove compartment. I said: "Boy, look, the season of basketball is almost over, let us worship each bounce of the ball, all suspended 48 minutes of the game!"

They reluctantly complied.

You should see them eye the inner contours of the Pepsi Arena, Abe and Winston, Winston and Abe. Intelligent men becoming boys again. It is a grand arena, standing tall in the skyline of Albany, a great place to be after being cooped up like chickens for so long. We were ready to give up the strongbox of our passions.

With sizzling pizza in hand, and a Coke for each, Abe noted: "You know this tradition of pizza and a Coke at the game goes back more than one hundred and thirteen years." Game-time is absorbing time. You forgot about Allison, her stepmom, her neighbors, your neighbors.

The Locker Room

It always astonishes me how Abe and I notice smells, while Winston is all thoughts and words. As we entered the arena, as all had to get into the spirit by passing through the locker room, we felt smell more than anything.

Besides the usual aromatic sweat-drenched green lockers themselves, each standing six feet and six inches tall and about three feet wide to accommodate all kinds of sports gear, this Pole team had a set of motivational posters on the walls entering the showers:

Tyranny before dishonor

Tyranny is tomorrow

Our machines do not lie

The Poles, "a debased and powerless lower order of athlete," were still willing to play competitions in crammed stadiums. This phrasing was lifted straight from a pamphlet issued by the State. I never felt them debased or powerless. Yet what the State said many, many believed.

"It keeps the bread on the table," said the captain of the Poles the week before the reopening, coughing. His jumper was pure—his shot cleared half court in a high-arced whoosh, both inside and outside stadiums, in defiance of winds. Few athletes had mastered the weather so well. He said all this with a wonderful Polish accent: "I was born poor, but in a lucky place. You learn perfect shot in Poland since it is so flat. The winds give you test. You pass."

His actual bio showed he was born in upstate New York near Potsdam, by the Canadian border. While there was no such thing as Poland left—it had shrunk to nothing as the German and Russian nations expanded—there was still a surge of Polish pride in folks like me, who hung pictures in our basements of the Old Country. On some of the old family photos, browned with age, my father had painted halos around family members of a distant past. We had pictures of guardian angels all over, from bathrooms to bedrooms.

Like the slogans on their posters, the Poles were competitive and fiercely focused. Their owners were focused, even more than the players, and they implanted a steep daily discipline into each player they selected for the team. The owners were a stern partnership. In fact, legend has it that their original company was incorporated under "Stern Partners."

The founder of The Poles team remains a well-known doctor from Vienna, who first excelled as a brain surgeon in the Institute for Cerebral Anatomy. He had made his millions studying the structure, nature, and diseases of the European mind; and he brought that knowledge into sports medicine and then sports competition. He did this by teaming with Stanley, a rare Pole, who had advanced degrees in the United States on the interpretation of dreams.

They had met while watching the inferior Ukrainian basketball team in 2030. They formed the partnership and began a revolutionary practice routine, playing hard in ill-lit basements, during the pandemic.

The Poles were now ready to beat The Champs—if those God damn American Champs were willing to play. This is not just my wording, many announcers now referred to them as the "Goddamned Champs." They called themselves American. This was suspect, but legal by State rules, since three from the club were from within the continental United States. "The rest are imports," noted Abe curtly. It was one of the many ways the Poles turned their ire against The Champs.

The next set of banners hung up above where we sat.

To murder one's memory is freedom

Trust each machine, and win

Reorganize for victory

Tyranny is one thing, but murder is another.

Tyranny is a state of mind, if you think it through, but murder is before you, evidenced. Were they really suggesting that, to enjoy a game or our future, we would need to murder our memory? When I looked around and saw the large clusters of drunk knuckleheads in expensive seats, I thought: perhaps the banner is right, but which preceded which?

Here now we had an aisle access to our seats, and only a few could see this subtle request to reorganize for victory.

I am sure these banners, which did get revised during all games, were meant to fascinate, and to confuse, at the same time. Flashing words in front of fans is a furious way to add social meaning to game time.

Meanwhile, the Poles pranced around the arena, and simultaneously on TV, and on Instagram. Winston noted that they acted dangerously, like that club in Eastern Europe that beat the Nazi police force in Kiev, before they were isolated, interrogated, asked questions about each family member, and then executed one by one behind the stadium back in 1939.

But this is 2040, and it was no longer fashionable to pause for the family lineage of the interrogations. "The State is interested now in deviant individuals without pausing to examine family ties and local histories," noted Abe.

As we contemplated the differences between the banners, bright yellow ads for "STORM TESTS at $3,000 FLAT" appeared. These flash ads—a new form of social marketing—flashed above the skulls of some of the players. This added new excitement to their ball handling. These were computer-generated holograms of some impact on the average human observer. For those, like me, who have failing eyesight, it looks like some of the players have a halo behind their heads.

The Champs

The Champs were known for their tender bravery. It took the stroke of some $2,000 Fahrney's pen to come up with this resounding focus phrase of the Champs: "tender bravery" and then countless dollars to embed it into every search engine, so the team and phrase became synonymous. Perhaps this came up as part of an MBA on Brand from Yale or INSEAD in Paris. But it stuck like shit on the Champs.

Their owners were on the extreme side of wealthy, cosmopolitan. These owners had some of the highest elevation numbers in sports. One popular commentator recorded how each owner of The Champs made their money in the 2030s claiming that—

Designed memories are best

It was a secret code, like the loaded words "democracy" or "fraternity." No one in the ordinary seats could tell you what "designed memories" meant. All you know is that if you can afford it, you should have it, like preppie shoes or ties. The secret is revealed to those that can afford the explicit fees, and the leather shoes, and the Fahrney's pens. In 2040, the teams with wealth behind them usually win.

It was a battle of worldviews, as much as it was a play-by-play battle of athletic talents. A battle between the rich and the home boys. A battle between the freedom of choice and elite selection. A battle between giving someone a chance and prejudgment of both results and destiny. Designed memories were best only for the rich, period.

After each championship, before the long wait between seasons, The Champs would offer to the press a "tenderness quotient"—50 free season tickets to the pretty young girl who smiled the best during the last minutes when they would record "every face in the finale." The owners of the Champs felt that if they could match that fan's smile with a posted snapshot, it would pay off for all.

The elite behaviors of the well-dressed Champs inflamed my nerves. The owners of The Champs did not want any particular player to spend too much time in the limelight; the entire muscular squad took turns being featured, starting each interview with either humor or humility.

The Champs spokesperson claimed, in 2032, when they were beginning their annual ascent into fame, that their captain was "a real mama's boy." The sports press claimed he still sent handwritten letters to his mother each day, no matter where he was playing in the world. St. Petersburg, with its long array of copper castles—a letter. Sydney or Melbourne, with their strong coastal breeze—a letter. Memphis or Cairo—he never forgot. Humbly, he said: "She does not like the memory of electronic devices, never did. I can afford to give her the best, and she doesn't want it. A daily letter will do."

Game Time in the Air

While I missed Varlissima during this Mother's Day finale game, I wanted to be at the game, so I could taste the moment.

Since kindergarten, I favored the underdog. I knew, deep down, that the chances of victory by the Poles were slim. I had told Varlissima that before I left. She said, "Do not fear, dear. You have that ability to recognize opportunity. They have a chance."

As Winston said: "The dog knows what happens when he steals the bacon." I felt Winston blind to the nature of competition. These underdogs had heart. They could win without stealing anything.

Abe, recalling my upbringing, seemed to understand why I rooted for the Poles. In contrast Winston sneered: "You can see their souls, can you George?" His deep cynicism, and over-education, stung. I could remember my past. I did not go to prep schools. I grew tired with his trousers so rolled.

This night the weather had been acting up. Strange for May 30; but this was 2040 after all.

March Madness had ended; the college boys and girls had entered a period of rest and campus fun. The professional teams were done positioning for the long playoff season. It was a perfectly timed game for the three of us to be at. We were rather inland in Albany, buffered from a storm's coastal intensities. It all looked good.

Abe had his pizza and Coke still in hand; Winston looked strangely content. It had a feel of eternity to it; or, at least, eternal recurrence. What more could I want?

We awaited the refs. Their entry was now accompanied by big band retro music.

During the seasons of 2030 to 2039, the league decided to fancy-up the uniforms of the refs. They became men of fashion, with color and spin in their designs. Some of the refs asked Eileen Fisher's team of eloquent designers to make them "their robes." As the State and the Event Police began to seem everywhere, refs no longer were meant to blend into the game, they were meant to be known as "the rule-makers of the State."

As we awaited the dramatic entry of these refs, I asked Abe what he was expert in. This was the game we played before the game.

Being whimsical by nature, he said: "Killing the deep state—crimes against nature—fishing in your area—understanding the weather."

I found this funny for a journalist—such range, such gusto, such whim. Abe has an apartment full of the tools of adjusting after a storm. From his ratcheting hand pruner for the fallen limbs to his high-leverage ratcheting H.D. bypass loppers, Abe was prepared for any kind of storm damage to our trees.

The crowd was becoming loud, and impatient.

I looked up at the large, overhanging clock. It was already past 8:00 P.M., the normal game time.

Good Friends Are Mysterious

Good friends, I guess, are mysterious. They evolve over time. They retain the ability to surprise. They remain great, like the Litchfield Chateau up high in the Adirondacks. They bring sweet sauce to a dinner chat, as if you were in the great Santanoni Lodge, with big water and big trees all around your conversations.

As a person preoccupied with personality, chatting with friends was like effortless weeding. I could do it for hours at a time, and roam and ramble. The flowers would bloom in the days ahead, and such is life, I would say. It was satisfying.

I realized how special friends were when I turned 50 years old—it took a half century, at least. Youth is wasted on the young; but when you have friends from youth, it pays.

Jiving with friends across a second half century is a super achievement. I began my conversations knowing they might be close to one of the last we had, but it lasted month after month, year after year. It was getting wonderful. I know that is not perfectly logical, but it increasingly made sense to me. Friends are mysterious, but over time, they become meaningful, your second nature. Without friends, we remain an island.

My friends could take me to a river that blessed my soul. They helped me tell death I was less afraid. With friends around, I do not have the egg on my face, because I keep creating. In the end, all healthy venture egos persist. By redefining myself in response to key relationships, I grow and change. I get a better handle of my own depression, ambitions, confusions, and loves.

Perhaps the sin in selfishness, such as those that pursue vanity, do not see this power in relationships. Social capital is infinitely more worthy than actual capital, as you can transact it each day, and it still grows in compounded value. There is a kind of wealth in friendship that is like feeling warm at home.

A good set of friends is like one thousand years of sacred music in your brain; Sanctus, Gloria, Jesu Christi, and the like. Your life is extended. Even if you did not agree with all that came out of their mouth, even if they were rudely secular, even if they always argued until you conceded—it was damn good to hear their voices.

Good friends, I repeat as I look over at Abe and Winston, are mysterious.

Friends Prove More Fabulous

It was now 8:15 P.M. The three of us are still waiting for the game to start.

I am now so deep in the anticipated love of watching this game with my friends, if the Champs came out wearing pink ballet slippers, I would still go wild. Give me a game, damn it! You can see why the knuckleheads with even less impulse control, after a few drinks, do such stupid things.

No explanation from the stadium officials about what was transpiring for the delays. Nothing is printed on the many flashing screens overhead. We assumed, like those more patient than we in the crowds, it was the weather. Such is life in 2040. Such is happiness.

It was Winston's plain intention to get to the bottom of this delay, nonetheless. Winston was a wise ass and, as I said, a very good lawyer. He stood up. Looking around at the burly security guards, I recommended he wait a bit more.

We got back to our conversational game: "What is your expertise?" Winston never would post his expertise anywhere. I searched for it all over the internet. Not a word. He did not engage in any social media, and kept his phone numbers unlisted. He would want to win every argument; but unlike the writers in this friend triangle, Winston had no need, or desire, to tell anyone what he actually thought. Everything Winston presented was a position to argue. It was annoying, but true.

Winston had resisted the memory devices, and thereby had kept a rare privacy to his thoughts. Even through his resistance to post his expertise, it is important to note that the information does exist, somewhere. In an act of friendly defiance, I will share his expertise:

Progress and power matter

Tyranny and its resistance matter

Spanish home cooking matters

There is something shocking about the juxtaposition of these three related banners, sort of like what the street artist Banksy achieved when he gave the bald, grand head of Winston Churchill a Mohawk haircut.

My Winston had a different kind of mud on his face from these banners. Progress! Tyranny! Spanish Home Cooking!—all muddled in the same clear argumentative mind.

Recently, in the last three decades, the historically accumulated rage on race and police brutality against Blacks reached a tipping point in the Big Eight Nations, first in 2020, and then again in 2038, when Winston witnessed—and he discussed these developments with me daily—his hometown of Philadelphia being mostly burnt down to the ground.

Watching that week, Winston said, in one of his rare moments of personal and political irony: "Hell, with all this homegrown destruction, maybe I should take up Spanish cooking." He had been a long-time resident in the Spanish Harlem of Philadelphia, and he dug everything about it. But by 2038, it was gone. Paella, not politics, was his game. It was the only time Winston put a Tomahawk to his head.

After divorcing his wife 20 years before—in the middle of a detailed frenzy—Winston became an art fan, filling his rooms with articulated nudes. These were carefully selected classic nudes; you could feel the heat coming off them in his soft air conditioning.

Winston took this hobby of collections seriously. While Abe was content reading the best newspapers of the world, Winston required high art. His scoped the shoulder-blades of the works with thoughtful light, better than in most rural museum. It was like being in a big city museum; nothing inappropriate, just all nudes, and many of them redheads. He treated each with tenderness, dusting them once a week. I wondered if he even oiled them slightly each week.

He was an odd duck, when confronted with how many nudes he had purchased, and from where. Winston never quite fessed up, as Tony did about his militant toys. It was as much fetish and fancy, and it was, after all, a fabulous older man's collection.

Winston even had a replica of the *Laocoön*, the second-century piece of a man, struggling with a snake about to bite his crotch. In Winston's replica, the bearded man has his hand back behind his head, signaling dramatic twinges of pain. The large encompassing snake battled a frenzied boy to his left, and the boy's frightened brother to his right. The anguished strength of the father gains its effect, in the lighting Winston gave it, in contrast to the exhausted relaxation of his sons, who seem to have given up victory to the snake. Winston gibed: "This is a warning to all of us. Stay clear of too much alcohol if you wish to stay fit for your family." This was the only hint as to what might have driven Winston's wife and family south.

There were nudes of the crucifixion. Olympia had a ribbon of marble on her neck. Venus was nude except for her sandals and pillow. There were allegories of passion, and of depression, portrayed without clothing. His entire array of nudes filled the tight four rooms of his dwelling with expression.

Why am I telling you this? Well, for me, it matters. Lives matter, but the way to support those lives is to know something about them. Winston was Winston and I loved him for it.

The Lives of Friends Matter

It was now 9:15. Still no official word. Storms of people had already left in disgust, a few spitting on the cement floors as they left.

One person shot a BB gun into the banners overhead; and was quickly locked up into the panic rooms at the top of each of the terraced seats.

Abe and Winston promptly left for their apartments after I drove them to my home.

The Next Morning

The next morning things settled fast in my mind.

With none of the usual morning anxieties to burn off, I realized, after seeing the bad parts of Albany again the night before after a long time, that our Stone Church neighborhood was a pocket of exceptionally lucky people, who somehow—often by blind luck—found themselves surrounded by wealth, time, and the chance at self-examination in a world where that was rare.

No wonder my game plan is pretty simple: straight ahead.

"The times with empty pockets," Abe would recite as if recalling a popular song, "the days without wine and dessert, the thoughts lacking hope—these all so distant, all so distant."

The realization of our gifts at home made the disappointment of the cancelled game recede. Fine books, fine friends, and a fine neighborhood can do that to reality.

Varlissima ended the next morning's breakfast saying: "All your game time chatter, George, leads to a kind of magical thinking about the weather!" She does not care one half of a bagel about sports. I felt blessed, knowing her, both because of the promise of the game and because of her rare and fascinated nature.

The silly battles between the Poles and The Champs seemed distant and insignificant whenever I was reminded of the manifest power in a good wife.

Part Two:

Friends and Total Losers

Chapter Four:
Winston and Abe

A powerful passage by William James, written in 1890, enabled and then enriched my lifelong friendship with Abe and Winston. It helped me first study medicine, and then, by implication, it taught me how to become a writer.

The issue here is of the utmost pregnancy for it decides a man's entire career. When he debates, Shall I commit this crime? Choose that profession? Accept that office for the state? Marry that woman and achieve her fortune? If you think this through, his choice really lies between one of several equally possible future characters of his self. What he shall become is not fixed by the prior conduct as some argue. Instead, in these critical ethical moments, what he consciously seems to put in question reflects the entire complexion of his unknown future being. The problem with the old ways of thinking about this problem is that man is less what act he shall now chose, than what being he shall now resolve to become.

This concept that life was an act of becoming—I used it through life like night vision. It gave you such a more uplifting view of yourself in youth and into middle age. There was less moving in the shadows if you assumed you were still becoming, as opposed to already shaped by events, trauma, and your past. This passage enabled me to experience several rites of passage in one life. All writers find a way to love the purity of their first memories, but you do have to move on, lean in, and get ahead of your first selves, otherwise it becomes all anger, and rage, and self-doubt. I wondered if I could have even ventured into my lives of business and writing if not for this William James passage.

Of course, life brings one a thousand passages of worth, but this one was special like my best friends.

Abe, Winston, and I met over a college class debate, regarding what exactly the American pragmatist and philosopher discovered in that passage above. It was not a famous passage, say, like passages in the Psalms, Winston aptly noted. But it was mighty significant in its life implications, noted Abe. We thought that first special day we met that we had found a gold-trimmed map of our futures. Within it, I said, you can see freedom and fate, nature and self, love and death, discovery and certainty—a virtuous circle of life.

This was far back, in the 1980s, when a Dr. Howard Feinstein was teaching a special seminar in the Society of Humanities at Cornell. His approach to the study of the human psyche, part humanistic and part scientific, became the mother of my muses for me. His seminar was a combination of neurology, clinical psychology, and intellectual literary history—ideal for my growing brain.

I was the only one who actually enrolled in this advanced pre-medical elective at the time. Still, when we retell this tale of our meeting, we pretend all three of us sat next to each other in Dr. Feinstein's seminar. I've told this story so many times to other friends and business acquaintances that the three of us can see ourselves up there on the second floor of the Society of Humanities on the Cornell campus together. The carpet is red; the stairwell old-fashioned, as in a mansion home.

That life-changing day I brought the William James passage and the draft manuscript by Dr. Feinstein down to Lyndon Avenue, where Abe and Winston and I were housed. We explored this one passage for several hours, over a drawn-out college dinner, and became instant friends. I do not remember what we ate, but I do remember celebrating to myself the discovery of this passage and the certainty of the friendships.

Thus, we have been friends since college, becoming ourselves in front of ourselves, which is always nice, and complex, and satisfying. Becoming yourself in the context of lifelong friends offers a special consideration, something that can happen even longer than a marriage, and longer than a career. May each of you reach this in your lives.

The question, "What being shall we be resolved to become?" was the key question before each of us in youth—decade by decade—as we faced the turbulent demands of early girlfriends—decade by decade—as the fire of ambition before us became more settled, and in some months, extinguished as professional and family obligations took hold.

It is good to deal with the things of life with keen friends around, especially when they offer material and insights so much better than yourself. With each emotional torrent that arrives in a life of isolation, it is a tribute to friendship that allows a floating to the top. Sure, there will be times of shifting voices, and changes in emphasis, but overall friends are the anchor, and the ballast that keep you afloat—if that makes physical sense. It certainly makes emotional sense.

The World at a Glance

We are fellow travelers in this strange new world.

Winston.

Abe.

George.

We read the same books, and differ widely in our interpretation of them. We see similar patterns, similar shadows. Using the rocks of our thoughts, fists, even bamboo poles studded with the nails of reason, we have as a trio resisted the numbing of our memory devices—and formed a secret three-way society to resist the obvious. In this way, we feel a part of the American grain, like descendants of Walt Whitman, William James, and Bob Dylan.

Abe was a newspaper man, even in college, always looking each day to file his finding. I am much slower in temperament and focus, being a book-length writer. We have the pleasures of writing at least in common: the love of writing, in fact.

Abe was more multi-talented than I. He painted the skylines of damn near every city he had ever visited, which neared hundreds. If I was a pawn shop peddler of influence and relationships, Abe was first class. He used his journalism the way Robin Hood used his boys, to redistribute truths, and to convey an excitement in the events of each day.

Abe and Winston. Winston and Abe. You will meet soon another strong influence on my sensibility, Uncle Finn. Finn is that something moving in the shadows of our friendship. Finn, the man who with no social intelligence, lived in the purity of visual memory—and looms larger soon enough.

I thought I came to understand the world through the eyes of my wife, my loving daughter, and this trio with Abe and Winston. Yet when we meet Finn, things change. Still, there is an avalanche of thoughts and events that must pass before this challenge, and before too long.

Each of us has one daughter. For Abe, his daughter meant everything. She is "all the colors of the rainbow," he once mused when she had just left him for the opposite side of the nation.

For Winston, his daughter was a creature of immeasurable beauty. There was a stillness to her, in his head, something that he did not want to think too much about until she brought him her own children. Winston needed to know if his daughter's daughters would be as beautiful. Abe and Winston were so different in nature—Abe about today, Winston so much about a future.

Whenever we began thinking too much about our daughters, we got a lump in our throats, so we didn't allow ourselves to linger for too long.

Within my friendship ring, I would think about three banners I first saw in 2038 that said:

Stop thinking too much

Recall disorder

Reorganize for peace

That set of three related warnings seemed to sum up my life to date: I had to learn how to stop thinking too much. Recalling the disorder of my youth, and the fantastic lack of order in my earning years (except when I was wearing the Noh masks), it was simply better to leave daughters out of all contemplations of fate. Better to spend each day focused on the value in existing relationships and the great exchange of money-making. But now that all seemed so much a part of my past. I was ready to move on.

The only banner that matters should read:

Do not bring dread into the life of a daughter

A Pathological Attention Span

Winston had nothing short of a pathological attention span, sprouting facts about what a player was paid per game, where he grew up, how many surgeries he had survived, what towns he played best in. It made the watching mathematical, calculated, and humorous, all at the same time.

Winston had a way of halting any conversation—any game in 4D—and determining what was admissible and what was lunacy. I was more somnolent in my thought paths, deliberately so, as the logic of lyric made more sense to me than simple logic. It was not that I was guilty of sleep-talking in the daydreams of my days; I did not suffer from somniloquy. I liked the jive and the give-and-take of a game, and honored the dance of dialogue, for wherever it roamed I found it human.

Since college, Winston and I could see the gaps between the propaganda of the State and ourselves. That awareness we shared intensely, but I could let it float, while you got the sense that he viewed it professionally. For example, even in college, we could tell how "full of bull any TV had become." Winston watched the demise of print ads and TV ads, and endorsed the trend to engineering web-based ads. He thought these more accurate, for some State-sponsored reasons. We first noticed this demise of TV ads during the State's reaction to the first domestic nuclear accident in the 1980s. The TV did not cover the reality of that event; it shaped our memories of it. After the reportage, there were a set of ads meant to calm, to reassure. The same in 2001, during the downing of the Twin financial Towers; and even more so in 2040.

Weather was the new fire from the innermost turmoil of humanity, and the TV lied to us about its greater patterns and actual destruction. Storms were a dime a dozen; and like tales of old, the dozen contained more than a dozen. Horrible harm all around.

It was the sports channel, or things like SteveNash.org, that brought real truth to the table, talking about the nature of competition, and about how to help kids help themselves that we came to trust in 2040. The rest was crap TV, if even in 4D TV.

Chapter Five:
A Tribute to Old Friends

I have suggested that Tony was that neighbor who was a son of a bitch, militant, certain, and dangerous. He was that recurrent son of a bitch who would not know baby Jesus even if He climbed up his leg and bit Tony on his crotch. Allison softened him.

Winston was a more complicated son of a bitch, as you shall see. He was my dear friend. Still, there was something cruel and difficult to handle in Winston. In that way, he was like his namesake, Winston Churchill, of whom folks have written. If your mind was a vital vessel, he could store a billion doses of vaccine in his mind, and promise you things in an argument you could not refuse.

Abe Was a Complicated Chap

For Abe, there was no clear gap between popular delusions and the day's events. When you work as fast as Abe did, with daily news to file, you can never really tell whether a story results from popular herd mentality or it matters in terms of history.

A measurable delusion of certainty empowers all journalism, in fact, when you take the cold eye of historic retrospect to it. Journalism is a narrow street when compared to history's broad avenues. Believe me, there are very exacting journalists, but they all fall prey to lacking a bird's eye view of the piece of history they happened to be thrown into at birth.

Abe was a complicated chap, able to be influenced by the intensity of the current news cycle. He is a prize-winning business journalist, and a social reporter. I read his stuff, benefit from it. But like Gore Vidal of old, he was stuck on the dock of his own perceptions. Vidal was a famous American popular writer during my youth; who, in retrospect, seems stuck in the docks of Liverpool or Belfast. He had access and privilege and what today we call "high elevation," but he really only could see as far as the docks.

Winston would rather reflect on long impossible patterns—such as how Jews achieved equality in human history—than look into the particular prejudices a Jew is facing right now in our neighborhood. He would comment: "Emancipation, namely the acquisition of key civil and political rights, was never a single onetime event, whether you are a Jew, a Black, or a transgender judge." That really says nothing, I would think. Here Abe agreed with me.

A game with friends is at least ten times better than a game alone.

Whenever we watched a basketball game, Abe wanted to file the results before the game was over, hating overtime, restless during the frequent commercials. He was all train and steam, wanting to get to the station earlier than on schedule. Every game was a new game for Abe, not a pattern that could be discerned. Every new game was alive, like the news.

Winston had a small leather notebook by his side, in contrast, to take notes on what had happened, desiring to discern the secret patterns of victory. The problem: after the notebook was complete, Winston would burn it.

I must admit this: at 75, I have an extremely high basketball I.Q., having played passionately from ten to twenty-five years old, never forgetting the game from the inside out. This gave me the edge over the lawyer and the journalist. This, however, did not translate to other sports that Winston and Abe forced me to watch, on occasion, even in my own living room. I'd ask: "Why is baseball so slow?" Abe would agree. Winston would chime in: "It is slow only to the ignorant."

This last comment by Winston reminded me of Tony's parting comment before he disappeared that day: "We will be back, like a storm. This neighborhood is too significant to simply slip away from it. Only the ignorant would do that."

On the Couch Back Home

The couch where we sat for the games was once full of our jumping daughters and their superabundant range of girlfriends. Now it was a place where we heard the hurly-whirly weather reports: one coastal flooding event after another, disaster upon disaster.

Winston reflected: "For most of human history, our relationship with the weather was in one direction. We watched, we witnessed, we received it without question as it changed. Ice sheets changed. Extreme drought, strange patterns of precipitation, wind, and heat that struck the elderly. It changed viciously, but our culture refused to talk about it. In our own lifetimes, we started to have a two-way exchange with the weather. It is no longer one sided."

Winston could cut your head off with such a remark. "You know, George," he said, "I didn't really go searching for you that first time we met at Cornell." He said it as if it was the beginning of a very long dissertation, and I wondered out loud: "How could this possibly matter after 45 years?"

Have a nice day

"It matters," Winston insisted. "If you do not remember when you first met someone, the Event Police will find out, and give you a ticket." Each ticket represented a decline in your elevation number.

Winston was seldom wrong. He knew the difference, for example, between ordinary post-World War III snow, and what is now called watermelon snow, where the snow looks red and juicy, and is bled by many plant seeds.

Modern weather used to produce watermelon snow in only unique mountain valleys in the Urals, and on rare occasion. Now watermelon snow is a weekly occurrence during winters. It even happens in our fine historic neighborhood. It did not make much sense, but it was happening.

Shaped by Events

Abe and Winston walked from their neighboring apartments to our living room most game nights. It was unlikely that the Event Police had reason to inquire into their behavior when there were so many other derelicts to watch. They had, however, always wondered if their lives had been shaped more by event or thought.

We carried this debate about the primacy of event versus thought into our everyday conversations.

One recurrent theme can be summed up this way: if oil is the very blood of the global economy, then shipping is the circulatory system. Abe loved ships as much as he loved weather instruments. Winston loved the power structures representing what was being shipped. Abe and Winston and I would review the shipping accident news to discern if it was bad thoughts, bad weather, or a bad series of events that led to the accidents.

Accident reporting was a major source of entertainment by 2040, for both the rich and the poor, the informed and the ignorant, as the access to this disaster information became widespread. I sometimes wondered if it was all spilled out to make us stay at home. It was like watching and betting at cock fights. Whatever a cock fight says, it says in spurts. The same for shipping accidents. We know, for example, that by 2040 about half of all commerce on ships is crude oil, even though most of the Great Eight have 2030 or 2040 net zero goals for greenhouse gas emissions.

Are these pirate ships? I thought that, loving to imagine the grimace of pirates. Pirates were a personal passion for me, and these accident reports liberated my desire to see a Somalian pirate. Colette and Varlissima, whenever we were in the Islands, always made fun of my attraction to pirates.

"Are these State-sanctioned violations?" This question Winston contemplated, retaliating against the pirates of my imagination.

"Are they simply sovereign nation oil companies playing games with our future?" Abe's position.

We would travel the world like this by staying in our neighborhood.

On a daily basis, we divided the world like Stalin, Churchill and Roosevelt, by the whims and insights of our minds. Shipping helps us sort things out

Our Home and Its History

Varlissima and I lived on this old British pre-revolutionary estate for over four decades. Our original estate was once hundreds of acres, but time eroded the spaces of Saratoga, and we were left with seven acres by 2040. It was still, and proudly, a massive lot by most 2040 standards, when having a home on a quarter acre is the norm.

Abe and Winston were both urban professionals before they retired in our neighborhood; they were quite comfortable in clean-kept apartments down the street, closer to the Creek. They liked coming to our property, where they could stretch out in our living room and in our library. In fact, some days, Winston did his yoga in our living room, with classical music on.

Abe, who had lost his father when he was 33, felt his sense of loss had been shaped by thought, the realm of reading. I, on the other hand, lost my father at 3. I knew life is shaped by events. These were the things we loved to debate across the events and circumstances of our days together, except when the reflections became entangled with a daughter's fate.

We wanted to watch the games for fun and for elevation. It was more a question of status than masculinity. This was the only way that allowed us to be close to power, the power of the game, and the power of the powerful who watched the games—without interruption.

We were not bankers, insurance men of high elevation, or the women of fashion and food. We wanted to retain our influence over the statistics of the most important basketball games, if possible, and we wanted to have our neighborhood feel we had some influence over the outcomes of the games, to be inspired by their respect. For that, we were about able to do anything, except hurt our daughters or our wives.

Abe and Winston seldom spoke about their wives, both being divorced by 2040.

Less Smart Things

The day before, Varlissima had noted my desire to die at Stone Church Road. She said that in front of Abe and Winston while they were over.

It is true, although it was not one of the smartest things I have said. The first time I saw the down-home grandeur of the Church and the home, after visiting three dozen other viable options, I said, "I would like to die in this place!"

This blurted-out statement was primal. I remember saying it. It was as if a deeper self had jumped forward and spoken for me as I walked every inch of the long entry expanse up the lawn from the Church. The fantastic old line of maple trees, with trunks the size of a small car, spoke to this self.

I do not know where that voice of death came from. I was only 42 years old at the time; and now, surrounded by college friends, and our neighborhood, and all the books, I am nearly twice as old—alive in memory land. Why did I have such a silly thought so young in my life?

But even now, if someone asks where I will die, this is where I will be.

Over the decades this knowledge of wanting to stay near the Church brought dread to Varlissima. How could we maintain these structures? How do we finance the Church assistance with its diminishing congregation? And the gardens and old large maple trees—who maintains them, and our slate-covered home and new separate offices, as we aged?

Like a good Sicilian American, she was ninety-five percent superstitious. This streak in her made her more honest with me. She did not know where I wanted to die. It might prove an honesty deeper than any argument.

As we discussed this, Abe and Winston looked on in amazement. They actually let their jaws drop some, as she spoke the above piece of mini-family history. Varlissima never talked much about her Italian heritage so nakedly before. Her heritage is evident in her facial expressions every day, as clearly as Dylan is a Zimmerman and Orwell is a Blair.

Her hand gestures are described in the memory devices as 99.4 percent Sicilian. Yet this burst of family truth was more revealing to them than usual; it was the kind of thing she would normally only say to me.

Winston wilily noted: "If many things can happen in 42 years, many more that matter can happen to any individual in longer stretches of time. Take Dylan as my case example. He is like a snake, having shed skins to a dozen people inside. You might have to change your mind, George."

In response to Winston, I dug in, thinking I would die here with the renewed poignancy and intoxicating escapism only old age provides.

Winston was beginning to annoy me; he always has had that creative prying that annoys. Family privacy outweighs the reckless bravado of male friendships.

In the First Person

I see the intense connections in things, at once.

Voice.

Authenticity.

Sincerity.

Personal truths.

All more immediate, as on a screen, or film, or YouTube global posting. You can be a comic in a timely fashion and a chronicler of the horrid on the same day. I find the first person gives you closure, like a good conversation in a short cab ride.

Sure, we will fall and fail.

Sure, we can remain in a grand self-delusion.

Sure, I can be misleading you inadvertently in this style of abrupt nakedness. But you have a better chance of telling if I am lying. "More importantly," noted Varlissima, when she saw the weight of the third person lift from my life, "becoming a first person feels great for you George. It gives you a chance to see you and your world in a fashion more truly and more strange."

If the Pinkerton Guards of old kept their bank's gold hidden in the locked safes of rail cars going through the Wild West, my imagination likes to unlock the safe.

Let it all spill out.

Let it squirt out.

Let it wiggle and swiggle, vet and bet, brag and tell.

In the Hollywood of my imagination, wooden bullets spark.

It Was Elite Schooling That Blinded Me

Today, most people are content with acclamation. They are happy when their vote is kept to a yea or a nay, when their purchase is only a click away, and they click autofill on the rest. This is not what we were trained for in critical thinking, or critical reading.

I am the opposite. I like to elaborate, to fix a goal higher than reality. Screw this dominant repressive culture. Freud was right when he wrote *Civilization and Its Discontents*—elite training is like an ever-tightening belt around your temples or jewels. They make it hurt, slowly, like drip torture, and before you know it you are in the straightjacket of professionalism. Yet when in the first person, when alert, when mindful, I find that time is on my side.

Leaving these elite institutions, I became like Walt Whitman all over again, Ben Franklin all over again. Like a person, not a professional. And there is another lucky feature from college: I met my priceless wife there.

I cannot overvalue the honest kindness and accuracy in my wife's eyes. She can point out to us the subtle glory of a small insect—or screech at what she called the waxy, oiled look of the grease baby bug; as well as remind us, when I am being mean or aggressive, that "tact is the intelligence of the soul." I love her like no other. She never bought into the elite mumbo jumbo, although she herself was more elite than not.

My habits of micro-aggression do melt in front of her smile.

Intelligent Sheep

"Why does any of this matter?" Winston wrongly asks whenever I said, "I escaped Cornell." This really annoyed Winston, time and again.

And I am damn glad I did. The place was full of the bees of elitism; segregating me in favorable ways because I was a white boy and an athlete. Most of the blacks, and Asians, and street kids allowed access were, over time, cultured and reformed. I do not tolerate such nonsense. I repeated to Winston: "I did not accept that teaching job at Princeton before I finished my dissertation. It was offered not to me but to my type."

Such "self-defeating decisions" do not matter to those in power like Winston. It does not matter to the many middle men and women who work their way into some elevation by being intelligent sheep.

But it sure as hell matters to me.

How to Escape This Elitism

So where did I learn this escape route? Was I led by my teeth, like a deer running from fire? Did I escape thanks to the creatives—those like Fellini in film, Dylan in song, Banksy in protest wall? For me, you cannot sing in an authentic tune unless you've taken off the masks.

This literary cowardice is commonplace. "It is the last form of cultural imperialism," Abe noted. Once he said that, I noticed this intelligent sheep educational pathway had gone global, from my doctoral students placed back in Africa. You cannot resist the State when these masks keep you bound from your true self. Pick up the Norton Anthologies. Pick up any Asian or Australian collection of literature. In general, by 2040, many folks have become sheep. It is even worse in the realm of those who are not writers. People love to hide behind their handhelds, their tweets, in new masks.

What ever happened to this grand old Earth? What ever happened to authenticity?

Chapter Six:
Climate Change Makes Everyone an Immigrant

When Uncle Finn came back into the neighborhood, he stayed behind the Church in his van.

This was the first time he showed his face here, after the Event Police recorded his verbal fight with Tony back in mid-2038. Tony said they had fought about the nature and implications of Surveillance Capitalism. Uncle Finn was uncertain about the origins of the fight, and claimed: "Tony is jealous of my visual memory."

We called him Uncle Finn because he had a Huckleberry Finn feel to him. His did have a slight Southern accent, and had a skilled way of befriending folks. Besides his surplus of friendliness, there was another peculiar feature to Uncle Finn's mind. He was a visual genius. He had a pure case of photographic memory. I had never seen anything quite like it.

I once asked Uncle Finn about Chaco Canyon in the ancient Indian region. This was that ancient Southwest region of old America that Varlissima, Colette, and I loved to hike before the Age of the Virus. I thought of the Southwest whenever feeling frigid in the frozen North. I even read books about it, to keep warm, and waiting. So I brought Uncle Finn there in my mind.

I did not give him any orientation facts, but he spoke about the Indian's ancient cast copper bells, immediately, the only known metal objects from the Anasazi, which they must have received through ancient trade routes from Mexico. Finn spoke about their scarlet macaws, tropical birds from Mesoamerica that were prized items for high priests. I asked him to describe them, and he got the white beak and face right, the dominance of red, the long red tail, the twisted blue orientation tail above the larger balancing tail—without ever being to ancient Anasazi lands.

I pressed further. He described the Montezuma Valley as if he were there; he could zone into the ancient Duckfoot ruins like a Landsat military satellite, telling me about life in a mud house or life in a cliff dwelling. He did it so convincingly, the underinformed in our neighborhood could recount the look of the Duckfoot prints in the solidified mud they also had never walked on. It was all supremely entertaining. If you listened carefully, it was like entering the dark room of a movie theatre for free, where there were no censors, and no popcorn, just a fast set of scenes and related dialogue about the things most on your mind.

It was that easy to change the channel on Finn, as all the channels were full of color, delight, and surprise.

Uncle Finn said he was born with this visual memory, so if he hung out at the local Saratoga library, and went for an arbitrary stroll down a book shelf, he would recall whatever books he thumbed through. "It must have been a sacred birth," the cynical Winston noted. Finn's remarkable memory was a natural wide-eyed camera. This made sense, to Abe, since all great books that survive over time are persistently illustrated by great artists through the ages. Abe said on this subject: "Every generation wants to see the classics through their own generation of illustrators." I never really thought about this until Uncle Finn came into the neighborhood. He made the ancient modern, and the distant near, like all good storytellers.

Uncle Finn could visualize texts he looked at once, with little fault, but also with little understanding of the nuance of the facts he could recite without error. For the learned in the neighborhood, this created amusement. For the less learned, it created astonishment, and for some, it created caution. We know for a fact from State officials that Uncle Finn had never in his life strayed from the Saratoga region. And yet he had a mesmerizing ability to describe places distant and foreign with total clarity—as if he went there weekly.

On top of that, Uncle Finn spooked some neighbors because of his ability to recite passages from famous books long forgotten: not just the Bible, but also *Don Quixote, Pilgrim's Progress,* Aesop's *Fables, 1984, Gargantua and Pantagruel* by Rabelais, and even Lawrence Sterne's sportive *Tristram Shandy.* But for others in our neighborhood, like Abe, Varlissima, and me, Uncle Finn put on one superb show after another, if you looked at it right.

A Tall Tale on Top of a Ladder

The first time I encountered Finn, something he did raised my eyebrow to the top of my forehead. I felt puzzled, pleased, and amazed at the same time.

This was during a time when we were having work done on our home. Three contractors were way up on a dangerous ladder, and came down as I was walking down the long driveway to get the mail.

David, the skilled contractor, called out to me, "I have something to tell you George. It was very funny. This old guy I never saw before on your property came up to us, exactly when we were about to set a time-sensitive piece of glued window repair high up on the apex of the second floor."

I asked what he had wanted.

David said: "He wanted to bum a cigarette. This was very funny because none of us on the crew smoke. We are very proud of that. But I guess your uncle felt at home asking for one."

I said. "He is not my uncle."

David laughed again, saying: "Well he certainly acted like one. He assumed everything, and took nothing, like an uncle at home with his family."

Thus began the magical mystery visits of Uncle Finn to the neighborhood. He was Huckleberry Finn all over again, but without the youthful innocence.

We asked the Church mothers and fathers about Finn.

After a pensive pause, they waved their hands, with passionate abandon, saying: "Nothing to worry about that man. We've known him as a part of the congregation for years. He fell upon some hard times when his only son threw him out of his house in town."

The head Deacon continued: "We are giving him some temporary help by letting him park behind the Church. Only a night to catch some winks in his van. Is that okay with you two?"

The Deacon's wife added: "Please do not report him to the Event Police."

The Town Register and Uncle Finn

Simultaneous with these visits by Uncle Finn, the authorities had issued a moratorium on social drinking.

The State street banners read that they had done all this "to extend the lives of the people." From Europa to the United Americas, the Big Eight Nations uniformly enforced this moratorium, after they found it worked experimentally in London.

From 2038 onwards until 2040, London had reverted after the Virus into a smaller place. It had become, like Paris and Baltimore, a smaller, darker cluster of sick or well neighborhoods. The great London of old had shrunk both in population and splendor. Year after year the architects of the city raged with revision upon revision. But it was too far gone, slumped like the posture of an old warrior.

The surveillance software, known as V.33.5, was retooled by the State as part of their infrastructure bills to renew such urban disaster zones in our time of a climate-battered world. Bumming a butt was acceptable, although frowned upon. But there was no longer any tolerance by the Event Police regarding alcohol. Abe suggested that this new ordinance "may put the entire literary tradition on its head!"

Under the protocols of V.33.5, you could wear sportswear that explic-itly supported Unilever, Toyota, or Puma. In a matter of a few decades, the Fortune 500 had become the sexier Fortune 55. It was not only fashionable but assumed that those of high elevation would eat Unilever foods, wash with Unilever soaps, drive Toyota vehicles, and even play hoops only in Puma shoes.

Puma had squashed Nike in a simple Big Eight lobbying move. They had created the impression of performance superiority and right pricing by offering the State a deal. They had received Big Eight approval after their global "The Three Nations and Their Labor and Sneakers Campaign," where sneakers were made alongside teaching centers. The genius of this PR battle was to offer on-site training as you increased your manufacturing prowess across the globe. By teaming their product campaign with the need to bring climate-resistant structures into schools around the globe, they were doing a certain good and, thereby, eliminating "the more selfish competitors."

The appearance of social marketing for the public good was the most reliable way for corporations to gain approval for further consolidation; and by 2040, this was universally common. Abe was tempted to leave jour-nalism to take one of these better-paying jobs, but his reason and love of writing prevailed.

Grand public initiatives like *Inspiring Tobacco-free Lives* and *Tobacco-free Kids* were celebrated and elevated, while some back-door smoking continued. When it came to alcohol, the icons of Diageo remained banned, replaced by yogurt logos by 2040. "Without alcohol," one State report touted, "you can learn to weather your worries with a resolve of steel."

The town register, kept in public behind the Church, noted a curious recurrence regarding Uncle Finn's "confessionals" about drinking.

Winston reminded me how to retrieve all the data. The first retrievable record on Finn referred to July 4, 2030. His testimony noted that "In 1440, when Eton was new and founded in England for the bright boys of the King, they said a few things about not letting the boys drink. Instead, these boys were encouraged to use moveable type, the same wooden typefaces that Gutenberg himself had used that same year in inventing the Gutenberg press."

Abe noted to me that this could not be true, due to the distance of Eton from Germany at the time. Uncle Finn did not know that; but he spoke as if he believed his full entry. When he said this, the Church fathers felt him still drunk. They gave him another test, which showed he was sober that July 4 in 2030.

Uncle Finn went on in this detailed record. He stood before Abe, Varlissima, and me, and declared: "These days are significant for humanity, because once we knew how to cut words into blocks of quality wood, we were able to start sharing wisdom amongst more and more townsfolk. That worried the old Church, and it now worries the State. While few could read back in the day, these illustrated books were the ones that mattered for civilization. In a way, TV does the same thing for me. Damn it, State Hate comes from here. What is wrong with having a beer, as history flashes through my skull, and I am watching TV."

We asked him a few polite questions about "State Hate," and he continued: "From the magic in stones at the Maya locations to the mystical ridges of stone in Malta and those buried outside of Stonehenge in England, life is meaningless without illustrated books." We were puzzled. That night we consulted the public records. There were a few marginal comments by a local doctor saying, "Uncle Finn's fantastic musing about books amuse; but we are concerned about the slippery stone jumps in his logic." This was the beginning of a long slope downwards for Finn.

The Elevation System

Uncle Finn was an odd dog, for sure. He had a strange intensity in his eyes. He'd look hard at a feature before him, of a person or a thing, and with his arms folded together, he'd stand there for a long time, his bald head gathering dust. Then he would recite a long passage.

He also had an uncanny way of anticipating new emerging polices from the State. During the late 2030s, the State started a new "Height for Heroes" social elevation system. I noticed it had entrenched itself into all Eight Nations by 2038 as universal policy. The record showed Finn first mentioned a reward system based on elevation of the individual in 2035, a few years ahead of announced policy realities.

How did he know this? Nothing explained this to us in the records, even though Abe used one search engine, and I used the other domineering one. Nothing connected Finn to this implementation of our now dominant social elevation system.

By now, the numbers in the elevation system range from 1 to 451, each associated with a corporate icon. If you are an elevated citizen, you can go up to the 120th floor of any skyscraper without showing three forms of ID, you can fly across continents at discounts, your seats in the theater are in the first two rows, no matter when you arrive. You are guaranteed six feet apart from the droplets of any human near you in public or private seating.

Humanity's recorded minorities (now 83 percent of the Big Eight population) have low elevation, even after they won prominent roles in politics and local roles in business. Even Winston did not try to explain that development by 2040.

You even got free popcorn if you are elevated at the movies.

This elevation system became part of the new Global Security system last November—the system used by the elites to get between the Big Eight nations—and this, too, had been anticipated by Uncle Finn.

The records you can search on the internet, at least those downloadable in our neighborhood, point to Uncle Finn as a "predictive lunatic" but do not connect him to elevation theory or practice at all. He had predicted that our old social security system, based on nation states and an individual's hard work, would be globalized. He was right.

But how was he right? He was not a freemason, nor a captured servant. He was simply Uncle Finn.

There was plenty of local lore about Uncle Finn's incredible memory for nonsense. Idiot savants are found in all nations, part of the genetics of the random, the medical experts declared. But this kind of ominous predictive ability was highly suspect—"As it should be," noted Winston.

Abe, with his journalistic, instrumental mind, always kept his focus on the weather, not wanting any of his predictive powers to approach society or the individual—"To steer clear of the mess." Yet Uncle Finn was different from most of us.

He seemed oblivious to the consequence of his spouting forth. Varlissima noted: "He seems to spout like a gargoyle at a European or urban church, whenever it rains. He cannot stop the spouting."

I once asked Finn how he saw all these things in advance. He said it was "for the edification of the masses."

You could listen to Uncle for hours, and miss all your important phone appointments.

In researching Uncle Finn, a few neighbors mentioned a kind of "quiet mania," where he would go off the deep end and say things like: "With method, careful intelligence, and persistent courage, folks like me will check those bastards trying to weaken human memory." I found that rather reasonable but, for social reasons, was not able to say that out loud. I remain observant, but also neighborly. These neighbors could tolerate his rants about Paris or about nonsense, but when it came to his ominous hints of some obligation a person might assume, they got worried for him.

I suggested to Uncle Finn that perhaps he should keep his comments to the past, displaying his vast knowledge of keyhole-shaped Mesa Verde kiva rooms, or perhaps he could really draw out a tale about those stone slab-based walls at the Duckfoot ruins. I was curious what might be on them after all these centuries. But he did not repress any of his surplus memory; it kept pouring out like a spout capturing rain.

And still, there was a kind of quiet mania in most of his visits with us at our home. He seemed hypersensitive, and hyper alert. Noticing my wife had a picture of her great grandmother in Sicily weaving a lace gift, he said: "I learned that was done in places like Gangi and Palermo, this lace gift, whenever a Mafia hit man leveled a local." It was nothing short of odd for Uncle Finn to note to my wife, his friend, this unquiet piece of family history.

Uncle Finn could roam. One day he came into the back of the Church yelling: "We must decarbonize. Decentralize. Digitize." Simply out of the blue!

Stuck with the Age of the Virus, I found him increasingly appealing, even fascinating. He kept me from some of my books, presenting something deeper in its fascination than breeding and good education. His random genius was beginning to have me fall behind in rewriting my new book.

Uncle Finn sensed, I believe, that I was finding his visits exciting.

By the tenth time he came around, Finn had fully befriended Varlissima. She said he was splendid, like reading Frost's "Stopping by Woods on a Snowy Evening." "Finn is lovely, dark and deep," she would say.

She said he reminded her of the idle and kind vagrants around Yonkers where she had grown up. "Nothing to fear in that guy. He is all sweetness and need." Abe said, "He is a creature of utter solitude, who needs something more than a leafless day, and comes into our community to make music, and jolly, and some good conversation."

It all became a little stranger when I looked deeper than the public records, by interviewing some superiors directly. Two had instructed me to keep "an instinctive caution" about Finn. It seems that Finn had borrowed a bunch of tools from them to repair parts of the Church; even rebuild a stone wall that was really on our property. I went to inspect the stone wall. It was done in a shoddy fashion; not anything like the work of an experienced mason.

Generosity of any sort must still respect private property. Most in the neighborhood found this a higher fact, like coming across chapter five in John Locke's great lasting book on the subject of property and good governance.

Out of curiosity, I asked Finn if he could recite the passages on the primacy of private property in Locke's *Treatise*, and he could! But he did not seem to have an inch of respect for private property, even knowing its most articulate origins.

Scraps of Insight

Finn often arrived to the neighborhood as the sun was setting, another requirement of the Church fathers. It pays to be civil and to be generous, but when folks only arrive as night descends, it causes some disharmony in certain neighborhoods.

One day after morning, I found he had left behind a single sheet of paper in his old-fashioned handwriting. It said:

Historical Figures
From early rulers like George Washington, and his brilliant deputies, to philosophers and revolutionaries, our neighborhood joins personalities that shaped our world today.

The Growth of Civilization
Come into this Church to explore the progress of humanity from the migrations of pre-revolutionary times to the first manned space flights to the Age of the Virus.

Decisive Moments
Follow the earth-shattering revolutions of the nation, from right here,

and the major achievements of 2040 science and technology, and the milestones of the literary arts.

Key Themes

Discover the common threads that join this special neighborhood to the world's diverse and distant cultures, as well as their knowable differences.

The sheet was laminated. It was spaced perfectly, with care.

I sat there stunned. Was this the writing of a would-be Saratoga realtor, selling the attributes of our special neighborhood to an outside coalition of the willing? Or was this a man who found a sheet of paper on the streets of Saratoga and copied it in his own script?

The more I talked about Finn to the neighbors, the more I could not guess. The reactions were both mixed and fascinating.

There was something about the sheet of paper that bent time. The way it positioned the neighborhood in the greater scale of things was quite clever. He could bring in the past with the present, the precise with the grand.

I knew this laminated sheet was his own handwriting, for Finn had often left little notes to Varlissima on the side step of our home by the flower pots up our back steps. These scrap notes were both private and peering. They were terse, somber really, very different from the laminated sheet he'd left behind that day. I found them fascinating.

Here Finn reminded me of an experience I had in youth. Growing up rather poor, we did not have anything but a shallow crawl space beneath my bedroom, which I shared with foster children. Each morning a rabbit, inhabiting a spot in that basement that was warm, would jump up and hit its head—Thump. Thump. Thump—its way of holding on to existence, waking all of us up. Finn was exactly like that rabbit of my youth.

I had never seen anything like this from my days as a reader in high school, the long decade of training at Cornell, or since. I never encountered before a person so bizarre and appealing.

In an odd way, Uncle Finn reminded me of my days on the basketball court, where I found loonies and crazies might have a fine shot but a poor verbal brain. They would spout nonsense as they excelled in basketball grace and force. Uncle Finn topped them all by being especially and exclusively himself. He was a full-grown adult, but I sensed he was a kid at heart—and one who might encourage other kids to put their tongues on pump handles in winter.

If getting older boils down to having a very long private conversation about your life in your own head, then Uncle Finn was a master at interfering with and redirecting my life conversation.

One thing I knew for sure: As I grew older, in this distinguished neighborhood of friends, I had more questions than answers regarding Uncle Finn, and his fate. I felt younger with him, alive, in playing shape again, ready for surprise and strange moves to the basket. While Winston could bury any in an argument, Uncle Finn could take you places in a single rant.

What did Uncle Finn mean about connecting the neighborhood to the classical days? His laminated sheet was full of appealing oddities, and profound indirection.

If it was a joke, I took it seriously. Was it a surplus appeal for acceptance in our neighborhood?

Did a coherent picture emerge uniting all his stray prayers in line with the extended marketing piece about our neighborhood? Why did most of his normal scraps have titles and subtitles?

Sampling the full set of his written rants, I asked myself: Did they add up to a book of poems, a coherent philosophy?

I decided these were not wind-blown scraps of random warm air, but instead were parts of a deliberate and quite amazing puzzle. I had this experience before in discovering works of genius. When I first was on the strong painkillers during a knee surgery recovery, where I was then pumped with antibiotics after serious infection after the surgery, I discovered an excited brilliance in the scraps of Nietzsche's hilariously serious musings. The will to power—what a strange conception, really, but brilliant. Perhaps Uncle Finn was like that?

One long week, I assembled a sampling of the key subtitles from Uncle Finn's scraps:

The Books I've Read

Building on Fire

Roads to Somewhere Near

Humor During Street Protests

The Ancients and the Modern

Cave Kivas at Night

A Neighbor's Wife

Abe immediately noticed that with this range of concerns it was clear that Uncle Finn had to work daily at his trade to make such a corpus of concerns. "There is a little insanity in that alone," noted Winston.

How could someone of Finn's background know enough to suggest, in his longer spontaneous verbal rambles to this neighborhood, the grandness of epic poetry and the twists and turns of a Zuni saga? And how could Uncle Finn offer distracting scrap aphorisms, full of sharp thorns and briars like a professional journalist or comic?

Was this the work of a mind in distress of surplus?

Look at his almost paranoid scraps. There is both a naïve brevity to some of his insights, and a sustained intelligent critique in others. In this way, there was again both genius and paranoia.

I asked in my journal, in a colorful moment no one was to see: "*Is Uncle Finn on the High Horse of a New Apocalypse?*"

I could see at last why Varlissima was charmed by Finn: there was a quiet genius in this man, a puzzle we should have felt obliged to assemble as a way of better understanding his entry into the neighborhood of Stone Church Road.

I took my first cut at organizing his scraps into a personal portfolio, dividing it into parts like an archivist during the last frenzied days of Nietzsche in 1888:

Emancipatory Prose

Transformative Prose

Compensatory Prose of Abundant Recompense

Anti-State Prose Meant to Hurt No One

The Theater of Truth

The Power in Spectacle and Recall

Euphoria in the Ordinary

These seven categories seemed to organize the spillage in his profusions, the order to his madness. I wanted to review each section, because most of them struck me as earning empathy. Over the months of his visitations, I found other stray scraps his notebooks. One said:

At the command of the sun god...
may my justice become visible in the land.

Another said:

Trust the diseased skull of an Anasazi woman.

Varlissima and I found those combined near each other, although written as separate scraps, somehow ominous. The first scrap about the sun god and justice had an explosive suggestion in it that might, according to the rules, qualify as worthy of reporting. The second was direct and scary. Another tiny rushed snippet said:

Think of tomorrow; the past can't be mended.

I was beginning to sense an articulate desperation in Uncle Finn's musings, as if he was fraying from normalcy. Oh, that word *normalcy*. It is the word too often used in our annual checkups! And here I found myself using it.

Getting spooked about all these scraps, I assembled a notebook for our great local attorney, Winston. His coolheaded approach was palpable—the way he distills argument, weighs evidence, and rules decisively amazed me. His opinion on Finn would carry some weight in the neighborhood. I showed him the scraps.

He said he'd get back to me in a week. It took months.

Asking Friends About Uncle Finn

Although we were progressing nicely into early spring, this decision to go forward with an investigation into Finn's standing brought some darkness with it, and a regression to the feeling of winter.

The Event Police would eventually catch up to him. It might be by mid-summer, it might be by the darkest day of the year. They would catch up. I knew that for sure. Yet I wanted to reconcile within myself something simple: what made this idiot savant tick?

I decided Uncle Finn was the best-mannered and kindest stalker in the world. After first discussing this with Varlissima on a long walk, I brought up the stalker theme to her in private. She noted that some nights, as the light dimmed, she could see him across the street, sitting on the stone wall beside the Stone Church, facing our bedroom window and smoking a butt.

I asked my dear friend Abe if he thought Finn was a stalker. "George," he said, "I was wondering that myself. I was about to ask you if you worried about V's safety. You get absorbed in your own daily routine; you know. Write, write, write! It helps you miss the disturbing things right before your eyes."

I was in the middle of a manuscript, so I did not want to engage the Event Police, who usually will take three to ten days of investigations and reports even on a minor incident, let alone a report of something that might be about to happen. I simply did not have enough time to support all that formal investigative hoopla. I'd rather watch a detective movie with Varlissima after a long day of writing about hope and progress and what's next.

Investigating the Weather

Time passed. Eventually, a tornado revealed all.

Abe had reminded me that what I called hurricanes in our town were actually tornados. He said there was a Fujita Scale of tornado severity, developed by the Japanese, that was worth noting, when considering how to characterize a storm. "These are clearly tornadoes," he insisted. I took his word for it.

I took down my large hard-bound picture book titled *Weather: An Illustrated History*. It proved my kind of book, both informative and eye-opening. I had never seen the distinct order and yet randomness of storms so clearly as that afternoon, musing on Finn.

I had pursued the topic of weather, and its changes, with Abe and Winston over the years. This book put some of our conversations into a new perspective. You could see fate and equity and fairness in the weather, as well as revenge and other matters. The book reminded me, for example, that water is so precious after a storm that it puts men and women on the same level as animals.

There was a picture of what were called Vortex Streets, seen from the air that demonstrated the value of appreciating chaos theory in regard to storms. A few houses saved, others demolished with the whimsy in Alice of Wonderland.

I came across a scientific excerpt from the book written in 1972 by the title "Does the Flap of a Butterfly's Wings in Brazil Set Off a Tornado in Texas?" The idea that the weather systems of the world were more arbitrary and demanding than the needs of nations began to be seen in the notion that a butterfly could create a tornado. It was noted on the news that a short storm could deprive a neighborhood, any neighborhood, even the wealthy ones, of its electricity. "This is why the world is moving to battery storage, and shiny new humming in your pants devices," Tony had once said, months back during that strange dinner.

We were experiencing tornados now near Saratoga. This was not Texas, nor Oklahoma, the homes of tornadoes during my youth. Since Finn's van was rather shoddy, and could be tipped in a storm, I started to think I could suggest that he move into the town's shelter for safety reasons, saving face, and not revealing my real worries.

I looked more closely at each page of this vividly illustrated book for further evidence about what I was witnessing in my neighborhood: I now knew what they meant by the word "twister." I watched the science progress over decades, but really never get anywhere near to predicting where these storms might land, and why they punch at certain places while sparing others. We can predict within a few hours now when the weather will get nasty, but not exactly where it would strike, and why.

It was Biblical, in a sense.

In 2040, I find it difficult to resist this sense of the Biblical, despite all the science and electronics surrounding us. The more science we refine, the more humility we need. I know, and distance myself from, the arrogant side of scientists and engineers. In contrast, ancient people like the Australian aboriginals seemed to share an understanding of the weather, as does Uncle Finn, who would often give some of the local rural people insight into when to plant and when to harvest.

While the State only respects brute strength and designed memory, storms did not respect anything.

"Neither Paris nor London," one of Uncle Finn's chants mentioned, "can talk back to the storms, tell them to WAIT, WAIT. The storms destroy coachman, doorman, scientists, and engineers—and any known class of laborer."

Uncle Finn went on. "They do the same to the rich." This was a most unpopular theme to contemplate out loud, the destiny of the rich.

On a human scale, Finn was the opposite of a tornado, which is focused in wrath. He was very much—in gusto and impact—more like hurricanes, very wide and disruptive.

With each passing month, he became more the worry of other men with elevated status. He became the worry of neighbors and the Church members. I told myself to sit tight, and wait. I had things to write up in a new manuscript. I did not think the matter of Uncle Finn urgent.

Booze and Words and Surplus Memory

Winston formally submitted his report to the Event Police later that month, under the subheading "Booze and Words and Surplus Memory: Case 1440 Eton Fancy." The casework was filed near the Milton Town Hall, before the supermarket, in the little warehouse where an old factory water wheel stands outside.

Immediately after filing, tons of additional testimony flew in your face, posted with podcasts. Suddenly, the net was alive in our neighborhood with accounts of Uncle Finn.

His expiation.

His exorcism, with references for the old Christian islands of expulsion.

His reconciliation with the State.

You could not brush your teeth without constant updates. The mere act of filing a case number creates a swarm of bees, commentators from afar on what's near at hand. It took skill to realize most of the comments were from people on the web who never even met Uncle Finn.

In nature we trust.

In god we trust.

In our computers we are entrusted.

Part Three:
Earth As Hostage

Chapter Seven:
The Trial of Uncle Finn

Chaos and Climate.

Tony and Allison.

Varlissima and Colette.

Abe and Winston.

A new manuscript due at the publisher, currently titled Earth as Hostage. I am almost certain, as with my prior books, that once it is submitted to the publisher, the title will be adjusted and made acceptable by some senior editor or owner. This will confuse and annoy me for a few months.

I had a good deal on my mind when the tornado hit.

The tornado proved my first glimpse of the underworld. Tornadoes do not dance with nuance, as the pursuit of atonement does in classical civilization. Climate storms lack the substance of teacher and colleague. It is all destruction, with little reason and moral. These storms are the swords of old returned, with blood spurting and guts spilling out. We have little left for reason before a storm surge of the size of those swallowing Japan, Australia's lovely coast, and my Long Island.

Dante has too much detail on Hell. The books of old told elaborate fables; now we just have a blank screen when the electricity goes out. We are in a new purgatory, like that rare turtle found in a sick, yellow skin. There is no politeness left; it surrounds, like a visit from a tax audit team.

Climate storms show us you do not need to die to know Hell.

Women's rights, why Black lives matter, the ways to calm the streets and the police—all of these critical public concerns become suddenly suspended in thin air like dust. It has been this way for the entire amplitude of Colette's life, from birth, to medical school, to her current practice. I watch, with rage, how the resolution of the issues that will shape the very tone of Colette's generation never nears during a storm surge.

By 2040, you found the weather had a way with words, much like a titanic tyrant. It had a tyrant's irrepressibility, its recklessness, its lofty references to something brutal in the ways of men. Like a tyrant, a tornado is swift. Yet at other times, a tornado can calm down, and be paradoxical.

There is nothing slow and medieval about these storms either, nothing antique about them. Nothing noble, all blood and guts, spurts and meanness. There is no middle of things, no path up or down, just all around. These storms are like petulant children: they know the right things to eat and to do, but they act against these virtues. There is no self-control in these climate storms.

I have come to remain puzzled at how these storms close up time. Zip. Experts call this the zipper effect.

Have you ever had a large horse approach you from afar in a pitch-black night? You hear her coming, you may even feel her breathing. You can feel the size of the beast well before she arrives. It is the same with the nightmare of storms. We've ridden these storms for 30 years now, and never arrive at a new place.

Nobody told anyone to fear, everyone just knew. No one voted for this; it came.

Reasons to Study Storms

A central goal of meteorology has been to warn of severe weather before it hits. In that way the word should be spelled "meter-orology," since the goal is to get the awareness and measures down to meters and seconds. The purpose is to make it all understandable, like the simple beat of a child's heart.

Yet despite billions spent by our Ministry of Information and Weather since the Johnstown Flood, we have not had a big jump forward in our working knowledge of storms.

There was a time when we made progress in our understanding. Back in 1953, a military radar system left over from World War II had the sensitivity to detect a "hook echo," reflecting tornadic activity deep in a thunderstorm. That was a pivot point in man's standing on earth. That was the first moment modern man could see into a storm. Experts could see past the thunderstorm, into things about to worsen. Back then, humans were seeing into a thunderstorm with both scientific privilege and Biblical warning.

Yet that knowledge has hardly progressed in my lifetime. We spent the time fighting over whether the changes were man-made or not, and did not level a response to the face of the changes themselves.

"It was pure, unadulterated political lunacy," noted the savvy Abe.

"They were trying to deny the science of weather," said Varlissima, "as if you could put a magic marker to the path of a storm and call it abated."

"All will prove safe," noted Winston, without reason or argument.

We can do rather remarkable advanced analytics in global banking since 2010—seeing the pattern of crooks before the crooks know they are being watched. We have superb surveillance equipment tracking the highs and lows of most capitalist instincts, so that our authorities track failed states before they fail. Yet our technology on storm prevention or alteration is primitive, after all these years.

Why is this? We have dozens of ways to prepare but are never prepared. As Babcia said years before, "Truth decays like tooth decay."

"These storms came about because for years we had total losers for leaders; and now we are all total losers," noted Abe. Due to the weather, much happens beyond our reach and will. Ships, unable to outdistance an oncoming storm, still have cargo dumped at sea—fancy cars and superb fashion clothes. Planes are still grounded—even the best military planes. And most significantly, the common person seldom has enough time to respond. It all takes an intelligent form of submission.

Or does it? We, as losers, are always taught to re-examine the pivotal events of the game. Perhaps we are victims of thoughts that have not caught up to the reality of the events.

Reading weather closely, I could see that while the storms were becoming deadlier, the rate of deaths had declined for a few decades. How could that be? I learned it is because the well-financed engineers of the State could justify better fortified bridges and housing and office spaces. In some places, they included basement shelters, so survival was likely even when the roof blew off. I have visited homes in Pensacola Beach, Florida, where the house is eradicated once every three years, and the insurance coverage allows them to rebuild the next month.

Only My Oaks Stand Tall

With all these losers and falsities before me, I went again to the wisdom in my backyard.

There are a few human achievements that withstand storms. My favorite are the oaks on my property. I call them the oaks of liberty. They are six feet wide at the base, an amazing feat for biomass. In a storm I can watch my Allium get uprooted and my fields of perennials destroyed; but the oaks stand tall.

You can see the oaks' pride. They do it on their own, over decades. I respect that, deeply. I had noticed that one of the things Uncle Finn did upon returning to the Church was to take in an eyeful of these oaks, and smile. I have to say, I never noticed Tony do that even once, back when he was in the neighborhood. His eyes stayed focused on people he suspected.

Today we have 32 of these grand oaks still standing tall on Stone Church road, more than half on our property alone. I have called one the money tree, which made my daughter laugh during her youth—another set of oaks I named after each of my books. I love them, withstanding all.

One morning Abe walked over to convey this simple observation: "It is possible that the pre-Revolutionary neighborhood around your home planted these oaks in 1760; and that some of those still standing near were tall already when the last stones of the church were being fixed in 1826."

The thought had never crossed my mind before. That is what Varlissima and I loved about Abe: his thoughtfulness.

Protecting a Classic

After inspecting my oaks and my fields, taking in the damage from the tornado, and determining what would need to be rebuilt, I checked in with my friends. All fine. Quite a miracle, really.

Strangely enough, I then asked myself if there were perhaps some way I could help "rebuild" Finn: make him into everything he was, minus the stalker part, which scared me and others.

Rebuilding someone's psyche to make them more acceptable in a neighborhood is a noble, and common, cause. Yet in Uncle Finn's case no one, except me, felt it a worthy one.

Perhaps I could tell him, after pulling him into the shadow of one of the more remote oaks, out of earshot of all: "When you next eye my wife, I am going to eliminate your middle fingers."

Perhaps this would fix him up before the Event Police arrived. That would be paradise divine. It would allow Uncle Finn to remain in our neighborhood, at the edge of the future. I want Finn to remain, but not the Finn that is threatening.

But he knew me better than myself, I suspected. He laughed at the prospect of my rebuilding him like a car engine "at this point in his life."

Uncle Finn continued to act exactly like himself. Once the investigation began in earnest, Uncle Finn became a legend in town. Like Robin Hood, wherever he did anything—where he sat, shot, drank, slept, or talked about his prior big horse bets—legend was born.

If survival in turbulent times is the utmost testimony to nobility, Uncle Finn was our neighborhood Robin Hood. Rather than preaching about losers or total losers, he attracted our attention like moths to a light, a bright light.

"The Uncle" began to represent for me the humane assumption that life free is worth living. While the great pundits of our day were searching for inspiration on what to do with all the social unrest, Uncle Finn rested behind the Stone Church from 1826, with his Huckleberry smile.

Asking the Big Question

As the summer progressed, my knee was hurting for inscrutable reasons. There was daily pain along the IT band of the ligament.

One evening, during an intermission in a key basketball game, I put a question to Winston in a grand Parisian analogue. At that moment I was both a bit agitated by the knee pain and also somewhat impatient after all these weeks of silent evidence-gathering on Uncle Finn. Winston's favored team was ahead in the ball game with a comfortable margin, so I thought: Why not up the ante on the rhetoric? Why not ask Winston the big one?

I said, "Now look, Winston, my smart lawyer friend: Uncle Finn is like an old 19th-century guard stone in Paris. Can you not see that he is innocent?"

I went on: "Do you remember when we paused downtown before those elaborate stone fenders? The ones meant to protect the corners of the best neighborhood buildings from the horse-drawn carriages of the past, far less precise in their turns than our autonomous vehicles? You noticed their frequency first in Paris. As we travelled the world of differences, Winston, you were often our keen pattern-recognition machine, our eyes that made sense. Think about it. Uncle Finn's warnings are not vile, Winston. They can be seen as providing perspective and public safety."

Looking now at Abe, I said: "Uncle Finn is a beautiful, solid, old-world corner guard. Sure, gentlemen, he has some imprecise and surplus memory problems. These surprise our collective calm. And he is not worldly, do not forget. Much of his harm is unintended. Yet he belongs here. He belongs in this neighborhood. In our sacred Paris of old, we needed these black painted corner guards everywhere. In a similar way, Finn adds a kind of safety bumper to our brains."

The game began again. It got tighter in score and intensity. Neither Winston nor Abe replied to my earnest and sustained analogue.

The Storm Came Again

That night a storm came again. It was V after V after V: velocity, violence, then visibility.

This particular tornado asked me a big question: "How does a family survive? How can we outsmart its deceit and destruction to protect our family? How must we think about these events?"

These modern questions need a safety bumper to preserve the comfort of our brains. No one can stand constant rattling of their skull by the storms or by those giving us the news about the storms.

In most of human history, a few were powerful enough to shape the political circus, and predetermine lives. They'd select the rings in the circus, the clans of peoples that would be slaughtered and those that would be entertained by the popular delusions. Yet when these storms appeared in human history, even the beasts that were tyrannical had no trip levers.

In a time of climate storms, everyone is a total loser. This is what I was beginning to detect from the long appearance of the mystical Uncle Finn in our neighborhood.

Ironically, when I brought this up with my friends and my wife, Winston was willing to concede that it was the storms that changed political structure, far faster than nuclear tests by maniacs or dips in the world economy. Winston noted: "The storms created a set of legitimate and urgent questions that permitted the reunification of the Big Eight Nations. With all this disruption rattling the human brain, after 2038 a new governance structure emerged."

Abe observed, rather intuitively, that the answer to the new political questions of world order allowed the State to play both sides against the middle. Because of the size, frequency, and inscrutable nature of the devastations, they decided to regroup as one, sharing resources, sharing intelligence on the path of the weather and storms. This was the most important world development since World War II, all because of storms.

"To hell with the local skirmishes," noted Varlissima, "let's strive to keep our eyes on the big picture. What is happening to our nature itself?" Once again, her wisdom silenced me.

I wrote in my journal after this exchange between friends: "When storms make the earth hostage, now we need to stand tall against the storms. We need to dig deep into this, and rediscover the rage humans once felt in seeking our basic survival skills."

With the trial of Uncle Finn before us, these new worries fell on deaf ears. This was not just Scotch mist before our eyes, nor the by-thoughts of great Scottish whiskies. It was an entirely new set of worries that had little to do with our *natura* as friends.

Being Biblical by nature, I strove to understand in my journals how all of this related to Genesis, Exodus, ancient Israel, and the New Testament. I failed to make the connections before the lights went out.

Reasons to Remain United

In the old days, politicians had to play the game of persistence: "Would you like green eggs and ham? Here or there? In a house or with a mouse?" But climate storms shortened the process, and tons of green eggs and ham fell to the ground, making it all reunite in a grand "yes." We will unite, you will obey! Otherwise starve in your differences.

For the first time in human history, an international agreement with teeth arose before the nations. Because of the devastating frequency of these storms, the Big Eight each appointed a new type of government official. Above the elected Presidents (of Europa, Americas, Africana, Asia Minor and Major, Oceania The Entire, Australia of Old, and The Mix of Flooded Islands), each of the Eight appointed a Chief Corporate Officer. This was by selection, not election. The CCO was the commanding officer in charge, for we were in a state of permanent war against the changing weather. The CCO gave us tons of flashlights, and a briefing of propaganda on how to "enjoy the storms in your basements."

It was united and all built-in. By neglecting the discovery of climate change for 50 years, the Big Eight consolidated their power beyond science, beyond neighborhoods, beyond personal freedom. Adam and Eve, Cain and Abel, Abraham and Sarah, Hagar and Ishmael—we were all suddenly stuck in the same flooding boat. Isaac and Rebekah, Jacob and his sons, Joseph in Egypt—it was all conflated into an endless set of storms.

How the Big Eight solved the issue provoked prolonged discussions amongst the three of us college mates.

Winston felt that if a group of people became too transparent, too local, you could descend rapidly to what he called "The Valley of Treason." For select regionalists, he would argue, "The Federation of Needs" gets neglected by selfish regionalism. This was the path to pure anarchy in Winston's bible. He stood by his sword, immoveable here.

Abe was firmly against Winston's philosophy, and preferred what we called "The Mist and Mountains of the Soul." Regions had primacy, according to Abe. They always had this in human history, and always should. Abe said that a person is a person, and a friend is a friend, and that is it. Winston got red in the face over Abe's positions, calling them naïve and dangerous.

I remained divided, wanting both the Valley and the Mountain. I believed in personal piety and group worry. I wanted both order and difference, alignment and freedom. Remembering glory days in middle landscapes like Ithaca, New York, or Williams College in Williamstown, Massachusetts, I wanted to *live* between the valley and the mountain.

"Is it even possible for us to stand together after a storm?" Varlissima asked. This struck me as deeper than questions of mountains and valleys. Her comment underlined another unanswered set of questions: The questions of equity! The questions of fairness!

As our neighborhoods face one challenge after the other, we live on a roller coaster of social unrest about anticipated food shortages and sheer storm upheavals. Many of my friends now believe that the Big Eight CCOs like this chaos, they like the disorder the storms offer them. "There is a meanness in human history," Abe once editorialized, hinting at all this, without stating it, to avoid the Event Police.

Storms and Social Rubbing

During these days of turbulence, many are left clueless. The only ways to answer Varlissima's question, I believed, was to find ways to foster social behavior where folks of both superior and inferior elevation rubbed up against each other—as in a street-side basketball pick-up game. In my prior decades it was in rubbing against real people, not talking with the elites, when I learned something that stuck to my bones like a Whitman poem.

But the Virus and its return after storms make this "social rubbing" between the layers of society less and less possible. We are becoming isolated in pockets of the rich and the sick.

We all have been unhinged into smaller clusters of couples and families. I myself have been reduced to daily contact of four or at most six people, once having touched the lives of over one hundred per day in business contacts alone. Imagine what it must be like for performers, normally in spitting range of thousands. This is what led to the shrinking in London, Los Angeles, and Singapore, a kind of constriction into smaller groups, and an eventual disassociation of joy.

Facing these questions, I took out again my copy of *The Book of Job*. This time I ran through it while watching the early films of Fellini in the evening with Varlissima. It was Job, and Dylan and Fellini, that were making more and more sense. These started informing my protest song, a set of notes in notebooks, a set of beliefs that reorganized my mind.

Through the summer, I listened to Bob Dylan during each early-morning breakfast. Like a good dog with a bone, I sometimes woke up with an entire Dylan song assembled in my mind as I brushed my teeth. Somehow the combinations of Dylan and Fellini helped me cope. It was the wild in their inspiration that created a little wiggle room from all the repression, as when I was being covered too tightly in a basketball game and used a microaggression to get off my shot. When I rubbed their sensibilities together, I derived a position in my mind that felt free. They together were like flint on a cold night, and the campfire was suddenly aflame.

"Thank God for defiant creatives," Varlissima said. "You need both wiggle room, and giggle room," I added to the jingle, feeling the enthusiasm I once felt before a key basketball game.

That night, before I could fall asleep, I thought through these choices between social cohesion and personal freedom. Abe had suggested, rather generously: "Look George, write about these recent clarifications in your mind. Your entire life readied you for this."

I constructed in my idle imagination a most elaborate analogue, something I imagined Winston would prove unable to destroy. I established an extended Paris analogue to the history of horsemeat. It was all very philosophical, something I could never expect to read into books of philosophy, which I often detested as bloodless books.

I was pondering the fact that eating horsemeat was taboo, unthinkable, and forbidden during the heydays of Paris life. This was a big NO both by law and by the customs of the neighborhood churches. But over time, things changed. Through that, I hoped to reach Winston on the issue of Finn.

I knew Winston relished his French meats—from blood sausages to refined pâté. Thus, this metaphor would be sufficiently disgusting to warrant his sustained attention. There was no wiggle room in this debate.

Establishing this precedent on horsemeat in his mind, I would elaborate. In the world before 1825, Paris was the grandest city in the known world. It had supplanted Cairo and Syracusa of Old. Of course, no sensible citizen would eat horsemeat.

Then a French member of the health and hygiene commission, someone like Winston, practical and informed, announced horsemeat was to be fed to convicts and immigrants. By 1866, when the Police imposed veterinary inspections on quality and freshness, common folks in the numerous French bars and cafés enjoyed horsemeat. A few records noted the consumption of horsemeat in the Admiralty rooms of classic France academies.

And by the time of Reunification of the Big Eight Nations, dining on horsemeat was commonplace. I told my plan to Abe and Varlissima. "George, you have memory, Winston's odd love of meats, and preparation all on your side, at last," Abe noted in a polite retrospect once.

Varlissima exclaimed: "Oh God, George, blood and guts! You've got Winston this time!" When she said this, I could remember instantly what her last five best meals felt like. As I prepared this argument for Winton the next day, I carried it with me into willful dreaming that night.

I had the image of horsemeat in my mind when I dreamt about Uncle Finn making a disturbing prediction: "By 2050, all of us will be consuming insects for lunch and dinner. We will feast on them for proteins after the storms." I could see frying the strong muscle of horse flesh, but the crunch of a nameless bug was another matter entirely. "How utterly uncivilized," we all thought in reaction to this odd prediction by Uncle Finn.

I woke the next morning agitated about insects, and about my dream's morphing. I noticed every insect dead in my window sills—lady bug cases, the remains of others in spider webs. They were often noticeable this time of year, especially the ladybugs, but most of the time I did not notice. I did not want to consult with the Event Police to see if the ancient Greek dream book spoke about insect dreams. I suspected this domain was new, ahistorical. My dreams were so vivid, I could remember the crunch of each bite.

Lessons from the Storms

We were rare, a most self-sufficient little wealthy town after storms. The CCOs were always so busy with other larger towns, they did not visit our region much. Instead, they simply sent daily text updates on how many of those with elevation remained safe in our neighborhood. The numbers often looked good in Stone Church. Ironically, these reports leading to nothing ended: "Do not raise your voice, improve your argument."

Thinking this through one Sunday, I decided to make a sportive banner to celebrate Winston's birthday. It read:

Evil genius! Do not raise your voice!
Improve that argument!

I asked Winston to improve his argument on the decay of Paris. He and I used to love the gardens of Claude Monet's estate outside of Paris, and a few of the splendid inner-city gardens. Winston's reply put a strong stop to my request:

"The decay of Paris was foretold—you idiot. It was foretold in the apocalypse of the horsemen. The grandeur of Paris was the past from Louis Quatorze to the French Revolution. All after was farce and decadence," according to Winston's collapsing of history.

I asked for evidence. He said: "Simply look at the pediment of the hotel that serves as the French National Archive. There you see a bas relief of the Horses of the Sun. They are majestic. All depictions of horses after look simply muscular, like the horses of labor. I rest my case." To him this shift from the monumental to the muscular underlined his entire point.

Already provoked by the recall of insects, I persisted with Winston. I asked him about the fact that horses were not eliminated from Paris even today, that the Republican Guard Calvary exists in 2040. Thus, perhaps, *HE* did not know what he was talking about. I said it that firmly at last. I noted quality French horses were quartered in a regiment that carried out well-rehearsed protocols of public health and public safety in the streets of Paris. This was not simply pomp but also Public Health, Winston's number one position that explained all to him.

He paused, looking very distinguished and French, then said:

"True enough. But do not be fooled by this in the new diminished Paris before us. Paris is like your Poland, George, horribly diminished from their prime. They have become a joke in the shadow of Russia and the Americas. While all the young French girls shown on 4DTV are paid by the State—with gifts of silk dress and perfume vividly twirled before our eyes and ears—to be fond of these regiments in red garb is to be deceived, George. These horsemen in red are not really loved by the people. They are loved by the distracted knuckleheads as the State designs. That is why you can find these girls and horses near major sports events. They are like embers on the Fourth of July, fading into past fires. You never really caught on to what matters in power George!"

This ability to keep arguing is what makes Winston formidable. Studs can keep riding in winter storms. Athletes like the Poles persist. But damn it, Winston did not wither from any argument. "You never really caught on to what matters in power." Boy, did that sting and ring and stink.

I had lost again. Thus Winston remains, for over ten years now, our neighborhood delegate. While my Polish name means soup, his French name means delegate. He was born for this. While Colette might sound, despite her surgical certainties, like a delicate flower, Winston would always sound like a large book snapping closed. He was the vault, the safe, the system. In his hands, Vesuvius could not have blown nor Pompeii be annihilated.

In contrast to Winston, I am perceived in the neighborhood as the writer who roams in his thoughts, making magic and mountains out of tiny spouts. Winston alone shares his logic with the Chief Corporate Officers, without saying a public word to any of us. His strategy turns away from the formal support of the CCO. He alone may know surplus memory's formal definitions.

Varlissima and I wondered if all peaceful towns are structured this way, to keep the peace. There is an iron fist in Winston's logic, where the weaker twinge under its anvil.

The Precision of Night Vision

The latest storm was severe. It was not different, in our measures of intensity, from the last three storms. It was only longer in duration. By mid-summer, the storms of this nature were becoming more frequent. Fires were raging in California, Greece, and parts of Pacific Islands. Other areas had a surplus of moisture, such as the Urals, where the Russian people complained to their distant Moscow that they felt damp, "like urban prostitutes left out to dry in farm country."

Many Facebook enthusiasts posted any scrap of information—such as those scraps that condemned Uncle Finn—online for all to see, not only their friends. As the storms raged overhead, many distracted themselves through retweets of dumb messages from the State.

Most of these posting, sent in clusters during the descent of storms, are not motivated by malice, or wrongdoing, or fear. They retweet to give them something to do with their rampant anxieties. Yet they are incredibly incriminating. Many post damaging details in the anxiety of the storm; they comment on what they retweet, and it is the comments that get the AI machines churning.

They do not think about it much, the exact phrasing of what they post. It is all very fast, with misspellings, and a kind of generic anger.

One theory called it "the lazy person's way to personhood." In the old days, when many wrote books instead of tweets and blasts, there was a process of refinement in wordsmithing. There was a process of pruning that took place before the bloom of expression went public. Now it is all weeds, water, insects wiggling on the ground after the storm passes through, and a few rare flowers.

The Deceit Rate

A few days after the storm, Winston took us all back to the question of Uncle Finn.

You were often condemned before arrival in the public hearing by implication and patterns displayed in these pre-trial lists. Winston had a few summary PowerPoints, showing Uncle Finn both before in his forties, and then later after he was thrown out by his son.

In summarizing his judgment on Uncle Finn, Winston asked, "*What do we mean by the deceit rate?*" He asked the question as if we should know; and partly out of shame, and partly out of grief, we allowed him to proceed without a challenge for clarification.

I had not noticed the phrase "deceit rate" in any of Uncle Finn's scraps. Winston pulled out something we all had missed about Finn in our neighborhood chats. This was an example of something beyond pure evidence. I guess all great lawyers do this—format the evidence. It was a superimposition of process, which was, after all, what Winston was masterful at in his famous tax attorney casework.

Winston suggested that Uncle Finn was a fanatic, could harm and even hurt some in the audience. There was no proof of this, of course. Uncle Finn was the sweetest man on earth, we once recalled that. But the way Winston started this proceeding managed to divide the neighborhood into discernible fragments. There were those that disliked "the Uncle" before they met him. There were those who tolerated Finn, having met his strange charismatic ways and felt him neither evil nor harmful. There were a few like me who felt Uncle Finn enriched their lives with his curious flurries. And there was a large segment of the persuadable, on whom Winston focused the most.

Whispering in my wife's lovely ear, I asked her feelings about all this. I was sincerely agitated by Winston's moves on deceit rate.

She looked behind her, and to the left. She whispered that to her, this phrase "deceit rate" seemed like a State secret monitoring code. She cautioned me to be more suspicious of Winston "than ever before." She said Winston was pursuing "an empty ship at sea, manipulating its contents we could not see." I loved this metaphor from my wife, as she and I remain pirates at heart.

You ask this as we are landlocked due to the Virus. Well, our nightmares tell us how to proceed through the turbulent seas around us. The generals in the State say, "Ignore this and that. Listen to the banners." We ask: "Who pays for the drones that pass over us at night?" We ask: "Do we not need the light, bright and antiseptic, of pure science and good conscience to cut through the lies of our ordinary days?" Nightwork, you will see, makes all this realignment doable.

Time continued to pass.

Judicial process is not like a storm.

It is a slow, methodical process when a legal expert from a neighborhood is first engaged by that neighborhood. When criminals raid a capital, armed, and with destruction before them, the courts can appear horribly slow. But that is all we have in a democracy; and it is all we need, plus love and dreams.

I thought about all the times since college where I felt Winston was impressively persuasive, but unfair, to the person in an argument he had won. He was always about principles over people.

I was starting to lose patience with Winston's process. In my anxiety about how he allowed logic and ideology to triumph with fierce certainty over a person, and their visible needs, Winston began to haunt me. My lovely, near-blind Babcia could see so much more than the fierce logic blinding Winston, and his profoundly depersonalized processes. She had often told me: "George, the long shadows of history will leave you stranded in a chilly place. Truth decays like tooth decay. Live long in the moment." I thought her almost crazy, knowing she had survived Nazi and Soviet infiltration by the State in Poland. I do remember how long she sustained the smile, with her broken teeth, after repeating that statement.

It dominated my youth.

Standing Alone After the Storm

We are all alone after the storm. Another storm, and oh what a storm. It howled messages of destruction, and the crisp slogans of fear. Oak leaves whirled, birds paused on roof tops, babies cried.

Walking our neighborhood after the storm, I noticed the road behind the Church was itself rapidly eroding. The once majestic trees lacked some branches where the local owls felt at home in prior nights. It was storm season again.

There were thousands of bloodless insects near the biggest trees on my property. Colette later drew pictures of their ambulatory spray guns, where with more precision than a spout, they had shot their juices at the winds, only to die empty and exhausted on my ground.

Others were survivors of the storm, still on the march—these soldier ants walked the tree line in single file with a fierce certainty, their snouts pointed in the air. And there were the half-dead insects, prey of my birds and bats that swirled overhead for hours after the storm left.

I walked around my seven acres, past the large oaks, some riddled more than ever by woodpeckers because of the superabundance of insect activity. The Stone Church, thank god, was untouched by falling limbs and the floods.

Curiously, Uncle Finn stood in front of the Church, speaking loudly to the neighborhood. Standing tall, he was quoting Shakespeare from *As You Like It*. His shrill voice, masterly, spoke:

*"They say he is already in the Forest of
Arden, and a many merry men with him; and
there they live like the old Robin Hood of
England. They say many young gentlemen
flock to him every day, and fleet the time
carelessly, as they did in the golden world."*

Was Uncle Finn dangerously suggesting the storms would be bringing along looting? Was he suggesting a plateau of fleeing time carelessly as a phase of post-storm anarchy? Or was he simply downloading from his rich memory a passage from Shakespeare?

This recitation of the Old Bard, in context, was itself an act of surplus memory. Fires would burn, buildings would collapse, explosions would occur—nothing could be addressed during the storm. It suggested that all our best thoughts could never, ever keep up with the world of events.

This speech by Uncle Finn suggested that technology, and even tyranny, were secondary to weather systems that were near, furious and free. He was a profound man, and rather arbitrary in his depths. When I think about his shrill voice, it was like the jazz sound of a Charlie Parker, meant to penetrate but not to last long in this world. It is his atmospheric intensity that offers the insights—as if he were pandering to the present the way Parker panders to the audience—as you look at a picture from straight on, with all the action spread out across the canvass in a fashion more diverse and impossible than anything. Uncle Finn was drawing us a musical and rich Bosch painting, of the end of the world as he knew it. It was a bizarre painting, full of gloom and intrigue. Hard to tear our eyes away from it.

We had a preview of his psychological state, in Winston's PowerPoints, but here before the storm, reciting Shakespeare without a hitch, Uncle Finn appeared in a quest against evil.

Even though I knew he was condemned, I secretly admired his recitation, everything about it. None of it seemed hidden, or informed by the devices. In excited reflection, I saw it like a combination of Prospero before Caliban and King Lear before the tempests of his kindly mind. I felt like shit having asked Winston to start the investigation in the first place.

As Uncle Finn continued his speech, to all of us who had gathered, he spoke of:

1. the majesty of horses in carousels,
2. the work donkeys and pure jazz sounds of Christ,
3. the workman quarters of Paris—their smells and their grandeur of freedoms—
4. and he spoke of all of this with that glimmer of freedom in his eyes. He could create art on the spot, through words and tales. He could render us fable-like immediately.

It was all a mysterious jumble that he never finished—pure unadulterated creativity, with enough bang per minute to keep us going. It was Uncle Finn at his wild-eyed best, and it was more. It meant something to us, something deep and mysterious about the human soul.

I recalled an encounter I had with Colette when she was younger that lightened for me these ponderous days. Sometimes my past with my daughter lightens my heaviest days even now. It was a feast of a memory, again, quick, like jazz. I had read to her, when she was about eight, a short Norse Fable. Here there was a lively trickster god Loki, and she seemed fascinated on how he manipulated the public. He got the public to become a frenzied mob that brutally killed Balder the Beautiful, a man so beautiful that he did not need hair.

Colette laughed each time I came to that passage. "Go on, Dad. READ!" I can still hear her bold cry today.

But because of Loki's mean killing of Balder, other gods with more clout decided to punish Loki. They painted his smiling face to a large rock—another thing Colette thought "wicked" and "super neat"—and with a slow drop of blood coming down his eyes, his final days were spent captive. Until....

"READ, DAD, READ," she'd say in a loud, absorbed voice. Her call for more washed away any dust left from my business day; she was a pioneer of understanding in her eyes. She knew to expect the story to improvise, to negotiate some magical space between Bach and Wynton Marsalis—and she became, before my eyes, the improvised space of pure fable! READ, DAD, READ. It echoes through me today.

During the last stage of the Norse masterpiece, Loki leads a battle of revenge. You could hear trumpet horns playing in the dark underworld, as he ascended. He has left his site of torture by building an escape boat from the fingernails of the dead; and he manages to collect a set of colorful and odd friends to help him quietly float past the bare-breasted women positioned as sentinels. Loki wins back his life by killing the gods who put him into torture in the first place.

Colette asked: "Dad, can humans kill gods?"

I did not have the answer. She did not care. And in recalling the experience of wonder in Colette's yearning eyes, I left my anger over Winston's tricks.

Chapter Eight:
"Even a Walk on the Beach Alarms"

After a few days, I realized—somehow the tale of Loki brought my fears back—it was my remnant fear of Tony's return with assault weapons raised that worried me more deeply than the return of the storms, and the return of Uncle Finn. It is unwise to dismiss this kind of fear whenever it returns, without paying some consequence. Fear is fear. It matters like the street you are walking on.

The day after the last terrible storm, after the Utility women in their tight black silk uniforms cleared the debris from the road, I asked Varlissima if we could go for a long drive—to assess the damage. She and I are part of that clan of people who stop for traffic accidents. I see it as the will of God; she sees it out of a different kind of need I do not understand.

I began to notice on this trip a consistent Hate-based pattern to the banners on the side of the road. As I had not driven down to Long Island for some time, I wondered about these recent developments and began Insta-searching. The engine of revelation had become so much faster than just the prior year. They were as fast and as inexplicable to me as voodoo. I knew they required lots of ones and zeroes and digitization to work; but that is all I knew. The speed tasted like orange juice in my mind, without needing to know who squeezed the oranges. Boom. It was there.

The search findings were revealing.

The first anti-family Hate banners were tried by the Greater Italia Consortium in the 2030s. The gates of Monteriggioni, built by the Sienese in 1213, is Greater Italia's best-known mini-walled town. Outside one of its lovely entrance gates, the State once hung:

Unite all brothers under your machines.

That Hate banner hung for two weeks (actually, 13 days before the second Sunday was reached), before 88.5 percent of those living in these red-topped buildings yelled, "Enough is enough!" in protest. Our car's screen showed us how throngs of residents went to the streets. Knowing 4DTV might help their cause, they spoke to the newscasters in English, chanting "Enough is enough!"

Varlissima and I felt closer than ever after learning of this. It warmed our hearts, and our sense of heritage.

There is a small but famous longstanding bridge that connects the mainland of Sicily to Ortygia, one of our favorite places on Earth. We had held hands there many times in delicate walks since college. It was a sensibly romantic place, with sweets and coffee shops everywhere. Once the stupido Police tied a banner on the street into Ortygia that exclaimed:

Drink your coffee.
With your machines.
Improve your memory.

This caused a confused smile in the endless stream of international tourists. But when we saw it, it made us angry. The people of Ortygia agreed.

The Sicilian district of Ortygia is where Archimedes himself worked many moons ago. One historian thought the banners caused stern outrage in the town's population because Archimedes was remembered there as a defiant and proud watermark in their shared imaginations. Within three weeks, the banner was rolled up and burnt—another casualty of bad State reasoning. Good lord, they should have known better.

The search results continued to flow. I was beginning to detect a pattern on the internet. For the first time, the certainties of the State as spouted by Winston were looking weaker, more splintered per region. I could hear a basketball bouncing through my skills, reconfiguring my assumptions with speed and grace.

Before my mind, major focus phrases of my past were beginning to be erased: the big lies, the solid deceptions, chants like "Lock her up," regarding Allison, or "Build that wall," regarding immigrants, or "Storm the Capitol." These phrases, which had echoed in my mind for decades, were being erased by the new search findings. It was close to a machine-based miracle. All that bullshit of the past was being put on a no-fly list in my imagination. I attributed some of the good charm to Uncle Finn, and some of it to Loki.

Here is the bottom line. The State authorities got it wrong on their banner campaigns throughout the 2030s. This was a big revelation. They thought the typical small town in Italia was in central mainland, assuming the farmer backward; when in fact, the majority of the small towns are in the better educated Northwest Italy. It appears resistance to the State is correlated with rural settings and basic education. No wonder the State wanted kids to avoid advanced degrees, and "get to work." Ignorance is bliss only to those walled off.

Because of this miscalculation at the start, all the joint territory intelligence reports had gotten it a bit off, and that cascade of mistakes kept magnifying over different territories in Italia, until the terror of the State itself was being lifted.

The Eight Great Nations now had a historic problem with the core of Italy itself. Europa subsumed Italy, but the rural center had over

8,000 townships, where the vast majority had fewer than 2,000 residents. This is what enabled some underreported uprisings in the 2030s, where people took to their windows and sang out protest songs. Bob Dylan was everywhere in rural Italia—Fellini film festivals prevailed. The articulate protesters would sometimes go to the gates in the big cities and paint the hilarious image of a happy-face cop with wings. This became a recurring symbol.

It took a turncoat resident—a tall boy named Bob who wore his trousers rolled—in one small retiring Italian town to change many things. He was a college dropout who was upset with his family—so, without asking his parents, he alerted the authorities how far off their AI machines had become, extrapolating this after that until they had become absurd. At first they laughed at him. But with the innocence of youth, he prevailed. He noted that there were 315 small towns in the province of Turin alone. The State's AI thought it had two dozen small towns.

A few of the mistaken began to wash their hands of the decisions they had made that magnified the big lies in the first place. The total population of these small proud towns in Italia turned out to be greater than that of the 13 Italian megacities, including Rome. If you get that fact wrong—the predominance of small over large—you get all the machines marching in the wrong directions. Thus, "The Stupido Hate banners." They were black banners, like those common during Fascist realms in prior State governments. You would think they'd at least use new world colors like those you find used by Unilever in 192 countries; as they still sell by nation state rather than through the dull colors of the Big Eight Nations—which turn out to be hollow organizing units the people themselves mostly ignore.

"This sums up in one wonderful walnut nutshell how the diversity of people matters to our way of life," Varlissima mused as we at last landed in Long Island, my birth region, and a place that fires my imagination. This amusement is not amusing, it is fun and fundamental. "Remember the large of heart and the small in clusters will always win over the State in the small town," she noted. Large and small, inclusive and delightful. A real wonderful world citizen.

I was not so sure. I am not certain that Varlissima is always right—but I certainly sided with the idea. She is Sicilian American, and for this I love her very much. Love over division maintains life.

This much I know from the basketball court, as well. Prejudice is a profession for some, an ingrained and reinforced set of misjudgments leading to pre-judgments, and a cycle of blinding self-certainties about others they had walled themselves from.

You can be losing by 20 points in a pick-up basketball street game—until your prejudices about your opponent begin to melt, and you realize they are damn better players than you. Varlissima's loving willingness to talk with all, even conspiratorialists, even Russian-Americans or pure Russians, improved the chances of me not descending early into dementia. If you expose your mind to the new and different, you stay alert, and free. Look at the neuroscience: those that suffer dementia share similar if not identical brain scans with those who espouse white supremacy.

If you cope with racial and personal differences, you can stay strong in mind to question each download. It is a habit of the fascists, in contrast, to build walls between segments of people.

I hope I am not going too fast here. This all came to me in a dream about monkish monkeys escaping their zoo cages. One monkey looked like a Saint Francis, another like a Saint Claire. The next morn I realized the frenzied dream had blended into my fears of dementia, addiction, positive addiction, and prejudice.

The black-hatted monkey of blind prejudice danced into the near blank minds—I could see the gaps in their brain cells—of those celebrating supreme power. Social history enabled those possessed by the monkeys a sense of power similar to those involved with narcotics. The wrong parts of their brains were lit up. In this dream, those centered in prejudice shared a sisterhood with the monkey of addiction.

After a few scenes, the prejudiced and the addicted both shared the same monkey on their backs. The chants of the monkeys had left their inner minds and began to be seen riding on the victims' backs. In another room far from the zoo gates I heard, during the end of this vivid dream, a small set of neurologists. They were studying how to delay dementia, suggesting there is a progression in the destructive mindset, from bad foods to bad thoughts. If you start with alcohol, sometimes you slip into hemp, and then heroin. One of the doctors, laughing like a devil, noted that these gateways have to do with paths in the neuro-mind the State now understands. She based her career on manipulative techniques to help her funders keep power and control. I woke up in a warm sweat.

At this point, there was only one thing to conclude, as I blended lived experiences in business with this dream work. The risk then is to become too serene in your later life. This whole tradition of well-being of Eastern calm may actually make pawns, compliant at-peace fools, of the powerful. If you allow your mind to fight the truth—through prejudice—you become serene, like some natives unable to fight the typhoons that attack their peaceful helplessness. In retirement, your brain becomes over-stimulated with a lack of new, challenging stimuli, and you need more and more stimulation in these self-deceptions. Thus come popular delusions and sustained prejudices.

A walk on the beach is far safer.

Fire Island

The Saratoga storm caused the drive south, normally five hours, to be seven hours due to continued delays from the massive damage. We took the bridge from West Islip to Fire Island and eventually arrived at Robert Moses

Beach Five, my favorite beach since youth. I particularly loved the history of the rise and fall of Babylon, near the sacred train station that connected my youth to Manhattan. I also learned, by living on Long Island during my youth, lessons about God's opinion of the poor.

We stretched our legs after the long drive, as we had done a hundred times before, with a long, slow, lovely walk on the edge of the beach. Dogs ran after frisbees. Sunbathers shone with the kind of oil that mixes joy with sweat. The salt in the air, the sun to our backs, it was glorious, granting us that deeper brand recognition that the words "beach" meant to us.

Yet as in the old classic books—*A Handmaids Tale*, *Logan's Run*, and *Lord of the Flies*—there was a rub where we walked. And it was not only a rub from the sand between our shorts! This rub was not as violent as *Clockwork Orange* scenes, but it was menacing. As every book grows out of what had been done before, every walk on a beach is based on your experiences on prior beach walks. You cannot escape that, even on a beach walk.

Even a walk on the beach these days brings with it alarms. The beach was littered with parts of a military helicopter that had not made it safely up the coast. I asked one of the inspecting Event Police officers what had happened. For a second, he looked like I had imagined Orwell must have when he finished *Animal Farm*, the fable. He immediately launched into a detailed report:

"It started when some U.S. soldiers of the 8th Special Forces group based in Fort Campbell, Kentucky, were ordered to get on the helicopter to assist Long Island after the storms. Meanwhile, this advance group was to be followed by a nuclear-powered aircraft carrier, *George Washington*, the third, also known as CVN 88."

I was beginning to wonder if there was an "official AI code" based on the number 8. Special forces unit 8; CVN 88. Abe once claimed that some of these storm dispatches were generated by AI.

The officer went on, like a man focused on both process and exactness, almost seeming preprogrammed. Perhaps Abe was right.

"At precisely noon yesterday, the tornado down here was so severe it lifted even the most expensive and fortified beach houses. The Rockefeller home—gone. The Taylor Branch estate—gone. The Trammell Crow Castle—obliterated. These Special Weather Force Agents arrived before the Green Berets—and like the Berets, they have 12-men A-teams. They dispersed across Beach 8 in twelve groups. Each group is oriented to a different region of the beach, looking for living dogs, people, and cats."

"Maybe the official code was actually 12," I thought to myself. We will never know.

After he had gone on in this detailed manner for a while, I wanted him to change his tune. I wanted to tap his knowledge on my favorite beach, Robert Moses Beach Five. He had the tools to tell me exactly what happened there.

But his focus on 8 proved unwavering; it was as if he needed to tell me, a civilian stranger, what he had witnessed.

"Most of the teams who liberated Afghanistan within 88 days back in October of 2001 had their genetics transferred to these new boys and girls on the A-teams. They were deemed ideal soldiers—having learned how to work with the regional warlords, they destroyed the Al-Qaeda terrorist network and pushed back the oppressive Taliban regime. They came back to Fort Campbell, Kentucky, with orders to propagate."

I scanned the beachline for other evidence of military intervention, as Varlissima left to scan for birds. He continued his report:

"By dinner yesterday, the Navy's special warfare command joined the A-teams with their own eight SEAL teams, five special boats and hovercraft, and several clandestine insertions. They walked the streets to prevent looting and other forms of civilian disruption."

I had had enough, I wanted to escape all these details. But he continued: "When I retired from the formal forces, I remarried a wife that allowed me to re-enlist to active duty. I continued to work after that as a beach contractor. And here I am today."

"Thank you, Sir," I said. "Thank you."

He pointed his long straight finger down the beach. "See there? You are beginning to note the communication equipment at the top of the USS *George Washington*." I did not want to appear devious, but I was dying to ask him why Long Island after a storm would need the full support of a nuclear aircraft carrier, so I asked.

"I guess they had nothing better to do yesterday," he mused. I thought about the expense of the entire enterprise. If we had only learned a few decades earlier how to seed these storms into a peaceful return to ordinary skies, we would not have to have all this. Even a walk on a beach now alarms.

Walks Keep the Mind Wandering

After parting ways with the officer, I continued down the beach, when suddenly I got a text. It was from Winston—Tony had returned to town, enraged. He had heard that Uncle Finn was given a leave from the shelter, and was once again wandering around Tony's old home.

Tony and Allison had not lived there for many months at this point, and Uncle Finn was totally sober. I always felt it pays to let your mind forgive, because you forget. But Tony had a hard time forgetting and forgiving. Tony was red in the face, and certain Uncle Finn would hurt the neighborhood.

I texted back: "Hey, Abe, why not get the Event Police to take care of this one?"

"Roger," he replied.

I did not want to rush to justice regarding the message about Tony. I wanted it to seep in over time. Tony was in a way a lone wolf, even though he surrounded himself with the entire pack of wolves covering the issues that preoccupied him. I could hear him howling in my mind.

The rest of the evening I could not get Tony out of my mind. "Tony really carried with him a heavy plow," Winston had once said, meaning he had one hell of a psyche. Whenever in the presence of Tony, I could hear that heavy equipment churning in him, weighing the scene down.

The Fear of Tony Is Matched by the Sudden Death of Abe

The next message we got on our trip was pure shock: Abe was, in fact, the first to leave this world.

His death was sudden. It was tragic.

He had come to be of so much service in his writing that we had not realized how malnourished time had made his body. It was sudden, in a sense, but it was an accumulated death, like so many these days. Towards the end he was living mostly on coffee, news, and his new deadline. Such a fine friend. I applied to deliver his eulogy, expecting to be refused when back home. They might ask: "Where were you when Abe needed you the most?"

Abe's last piece of journalism was called "The Carnival King," where he spoke against all the positives that consumed his prior ten years. He spoke about an elected President in central eastern Europe, who became, before the public, a man of no morals and all show, who others called a bum behind his back, an imbecile, a headcase of immense proportions. Abe noted how so many, nonetheless, admired him because he made good drama on 4DTV. "The march of time," he wrote, "even the march of time could not turn him off."

His final lines in this piece about the Carnival King said: "The days of the King will surprise us like a thief. He has made the heavens disappear with his loud, constant noise on your handhelds, several dozen warnings each morning as you rise for your morning coffee. His way of rule cannot be destroyed by fire; and cannot withstand a reform of the judges, since his reign is about getting inside your head."

I had that piece rattle in my days as we got ready for the beaches of Long Island. Unlike the "Lawyer's Prologue" in Chaucer's *Canterbury Tales*, Abe did not blame Christ for this clown leader. Instead, he blamed us. Luckily, this ascending politician dies after his first term, making lots of room for immediate return to reliable qualities of life and governance.

Chapter Nine:
Calm Breezes, Sliced Peaches, and Gin

With the beach operation winding down, we were permitted to wander around town. It was good to be back. Long Island had an open feel to me. I no longer knew who I was seeing. Time had flushed out most of the neighborhood. It is exhilarating when you decide to return to the land of the living. You start to bark at things, jump up and wag. It might prove a dangerous place to linger, but it is sure as hell fun while it lasts.

I revisited my childhood library. Re-entry was like landing a satellite. It brought back the hundreds of first books in my life, the ones that let me stand taller, sword in hand, with dignity.

The library itself looked closer to the water, even though it was still on Montauk Highway in West Island. George Washington had travelled this road when he restored order on Long Island, before taking back Manhattan from the British.

The library was displaying an informative feature on Woman and War. It started with a reference to the rebel girls of World War II, when Long Island women used some of their muscles in mines and munitions factories, assembling both explosives and arms, at great personal risk. Alongside them, female scientists took on the study of these dangerous explosives, as well as toxic chemicals, virulent diseases and viruses, even the lethal effects of radioactive isotopes.

I wanted to go deeper into the archive of the library, but my elevation level did not qualify me for that degree of clearance. There was a warning on the door locking the archive: "Wash the germs of humanity from your hands before entering." There was something deeper there that I could not see.

Unable to penetrate the archive, we returned to the hotel and replaced that frustration with gin. Even though alcohol was technically illegal in most rural areas, enforcement was nearly non-existent in populated areas like my hometown areas near the railroad track. Nobility of purpose is what we endure, and sometimes, a spiked botanical helps. Through time, humans have needed a few supplements, intoxicating elements of excess, to help us maintain our sacred obligations, the ability to care. Returning home helped me remember all of my earlier, more youthful decisions about freedom in the face of fate.

Sitting near my lovely Varlissima, I remember the day in 2024 when Winston moved into the neighborhood. That night I took a fine full bottle of gin out for a significant final basketball game in 2024, my best British gin—pure clear with tasteful botanicals. I also filled a bowl with sliced peaches from the can.

Winston said: "George, when I think of gin, I think of the actual Winston, the one and only—Winston Churchill, and his massive writings." I answered in a snide, Abe-like fashion, saying: "Hey, you have not died yet, Winston. You are still my actual Winston." There were a few moments of silence, and then he laughed his head off.

Varlissima was in the same state of mind—nostalgic. There were moments of sudden rightness in recollection, as Varlissima and I drank furtively in the hotel room. Oh, it was good to get dizzy together again.

Varlissima and I realized we had not had fresh peaches since the last pandemic. It had been impossible to find fresh, sliced, yellow cling peaches, my favorite. Instead, the combine in Saratoga offered a product in 100 percent juice, in cans, where you got a blend of sliced peaches in pear juice concentrate. Varlissima noted the slices seemed thinner than ever before.

Gin makes one realize that we are not fully on borrowed time. At my last checkup, my cardio doctor issued me an annual warning about being overweight. I'd let it sink in, but then resumed my lifestyle. This all felt Homeric, now, as if life was a long journey getting back to home. I could smell the salt of the Atlantic breeze through the hotel windows. All was well. I even forgot about Tony and Allison.

I checked: my heart machine was recording my descent into memories, calculating each beat with a slight increase in blood pressure. "Memories are good," my heart doctor had said, "but sometimes they can be killers."

Memories and Doctors

I could not really enjoy Long Island in that moment without a memory of aging. There was a book I had left at home that made me think about my daughter's aging, as well. It was called *On Borrowed Time*, and examined the ways that we die.

At the start of this book, a loud train of thought made me recall, completely, Chaucer's "Lawyer's Tale," which begins:

In Syria, once, there dwelt a company
Of traders rich, all sober men and true,
That far abroad did send their spicery,
And cloth of gold, and satins rich in hue.

In my life I had become rich, in cloth of gold, by hard good, good luck, and chance—and had given Colette the satin-rich colors of a medical education. Yet we both were aging, visibly. You cannot outsmart these thoughts of a daughter aging.

The woman who wrote *On Borrowed Time* was a practicing doctor. Yet as we entered a second and third year into the Virus, she turned from a world-traveling doctor into a writer of books. *On Borrowed Time* was her lasting product, a volume of real substance. She started her tale with the paradox that centuries of medicine had focused on the symptoms of aging: the dementia, the heart failure, the eventual swelling of feet, the general puffiness of that bitch goddess Death. It was all documented in her book with a kind of medical relish, the pear juice in the concentrate. Yet she wanted to offer something deeper than symptoms, the actual reasons we die.

The State allowed nine competing theories of aging. This struck me as deliberately complex. We age. Period.

I believe that as we age our memories become like horns and wheat and heavy things in our backpack, weighing us down. That is why many of the elevated believe you trim your surplus memories, like grey hairs from your temples.

In this formal, medical review they had authorized solution paths to each of the nine ways of aging for the rich and the famous. This sounded promising, but it increased the State's role in our lives as well.

As the gin started numbing my entire body, I could recall three of the nine reasons we die. She presented these nine as if written in stone, for when you combine the paradigms of science with the powers of the State you get functional certainties. Here is what I recall, again, without the book in front of me:

1. ***The Theory of Telomere Attrition:***
   She did not present this as a theory, yet she called it such. She was approved to do research on telomeres, small tips at the end of each

chromosome. She called them similar to the plastic tips of shoe laces. I have seen them under a microscope; they are life itself.

With time, as your body experiences the toxins of living, there is a progressive shortening of these protective edges. For some chemical reason (still not approved for public knowledge by the State), as we age and the chromosomes replicate, a few bits of the telomeres get lopped off at the ends. Snip. Snip. Snip.

Then, when your cells further divide—and this happens constantly—your chromosomes are further copied, but shortened a bit. In this microscopic process, the stability of transfer—for reasons still unknown—is less secure when we're older than in youth, when the replication is robust and accurate.

"Imagine," Colette had once excitedly said to me in my backyard—while my flowers were in mid-July bloom—as I was smoking a celebratory cigar, "Imagine what a full cigar does to you, Dad."

2. ***Deregulation of Nutrient Sensing and Selection:***
    She next examined the evolving and exquisite mechanisms that adjust our behavior as we make use of nutrients. It is not what you eat as much as how well you make energy from what you eat. Select nutrients in our foods are available for generating energy and the raw materials for growth in our cells. A lot depends on how well your body can detect which nutrients are available in the foods you eat.

As I sat in the hotel, my exact replication of her pages seemed a little more jumbled in my memory, so I checked my machine. This nutrient sensing and selection process was very complex indeed, as a peach is not an almond, and an almond is not gin. It takes a very complex system to select and to regulate these billions of nutrients swimming into digestion.

I remembered having a big argument with Winston about the implications of nutrient sensing when it was first announced. This all became highly politicized in the 2030s, when New York State had serious food shortages not only for the poor but for the marginally wealthy. "The State may have some solutions in reserve that are not known publicly," noted Abe. In an archive somewhere, it may be explained why the poor die younger than folks like me. Those reasons remain hidden.

3. ***Stem Cell Exhaustion:***
    The most significant medical discovery in the 2030s was about adult stem cells. It first felt like the discovery of the fountain of youth. Then our machines were flooded with the details of stem cell exhaustion. Now they have been taken for granted by those who can afford to believe in science. It was easier for me to recall the nuance of this death path than the prior two.

We all recall the debates in the 2030s about stem cells, those popular undifferentiated cells that are kept in reserve, like a bank account, for repair and maintenance of the aging body. Each body has them, but the great labs in Paris, London, and Stanford save them in batches like unpolished gold nuggets at Fort Knox. Stem cells are nothing by themselves, except when applied with smart technical knowledge.

After the Covid-19 crisis of 2020, our authorities began to watch how the Chinese not only stored organs for their elites, but how they tried to keep secret their stem cell labs. You have to ask why. Our scientists of the Eight States (excluding China) have found stems cells tucked away in most human tissues and organs, thank God. All elevations have them, in equal amounts, at birth. They are abundant when you know where to look. They can be programmed to replace lost or damaged cells in the tissues where they are found, for those that can afford the time and expense.

Over time, though, the theory is that even these re-deployed reserves get run down, and tired—in that way, their life extension is like a loan that ends.

I found the six other reasons we die beyond my current recollection. This was both funny, and sad. What had happened to that retention rate I was known for while pre-med, and during the early days of earning at my firm?

The gin was now completely transforming my sense of place and worry. The ideas of what kicked off this trip in the first place had receded. If you asked me in that moment, I could not have recalled the details of the storm, the military recital I had heard, or even which day of the week it might be. Where does that memory go?

There was no reserve in my short-term memory left. I went to sleep right in a chair in the library.

Monsoon Landing, Long Island

The next morning I felt great. Crystal clear, full of memories!

I told Varlissima: "Let's hit the town, along the small Captree Island townships. Let's start first at Monsoon Landing, then cross the bridge to Fire Island, and then go back to where we once rented a summer home with the young Colette."

Monsoon Landing (incorporated 1745) is a small Italian-like peninsula on the coast of West Island facing the ocean. This landing is where I had my first well-paid lawnmowing jobs way back in ancient history. It is a windswept part of West Islip, Long Island, where wealthy Italian immigrants lived with guard dogs, lovely lawns, and attractive housewives. I remember the layout of the lawns even today.

As a young man I had convinced myself, after a fabulous winning season in basketball, that several of these housewives would let me, with a little charm and persistence, cut their lawns. It was all a grand memory.

On this trip I realized that most of the lawns I had cut on Monsoon Landing were now owned by the ocean, which crashed inland more and more, reaching Montauk Highway itself at times.

We approached the home that was once owned by Mario Puzo, the famous writer of *The Godfather*. This was a book that became more and more important in the 2030s and now. Each decade made me think of a youthful encounter I had had with the author.

I remember one Saturday morning, after buying some bagels and Sunday desserts for my mother, I saw Mario himself at the West Islip Post Office, shipping off a package to Manhattan. He seemed like a nice enough, distinguished man, so I asked if I could have a look at his place to give him an estimate on cutting his lawn.

He said come by and "talk to my wife." I had heard many stories about how lovely his wife was, so I knew the coast was clear. It all worked out like a Bob Dylan song.

Meeting Mario moved me. It formed one of the cornerstones of my confidence in early youth, and through my days in college, the days daring to become a charismatic teacher, and the days putting on the Noh masks of massive earnings. I felt bearded, and felt like I was looking forward after meeting Mario way back then.

Part Four:
Surplus Memory

Chapter Ten:
This is My Home, My Neighborhood

You may feel we have a surplus of parallel arguments zooming through this fable. And you are right. Today's communication is about speed, multi-valent activity, and sheer visual entertainment. We do not have enough time to reread the 52 parts of "Song of Myself," or the many fables in Chaucer's tales.

Speed. Storms. Mindless actions. This is the fable of my neighborhood that has gone global, and gone viral, where everyone can buy the products designed by MIT PhDs for very low prices. While my memories of my past may now smell like a locker room, what we have left to say suggests that you are not as oblivious to the nuances in your neighborhood—the conspiratorialists, the big lies, the tireless computational computing—as I first feared. You can afford to get past the stench, and cleanse your soul. If this makes an alarm beep in your head, damn good, Abe would have said. "Read," echoes Colette in my head.

Varlissima always told me, echoing my grandmother, that you cannot buy wealth and happiness. You have to earn them. In this age of manufactured taste and purchased eloquence, it is important to remember to not forget that competitive frugality is attached to happiness at the hip. Sure, we bought a big home, sure we invested in plenty of education for our kids, our friends, and others we support. This is a part of maintaining the sweet tang of situational awareness. You have to invest in yourself, and in your commonwealth. Otherwise, you are like a pirate held at bay. The enormous possibilities of freedom do not reside in stated things; you must become your own observation tower.

I have calculated close the stray buying patterns of those I love, and my neighbors. I have been lucky. I have survived all these years, and been free of debt from the State and from the banks. Here are my remaining sins to date:

1. I have talked when I should have listened.
2. I have been hyperactive when I should have been tender.
3. I have bought a robust shelf to house more books well before I have given books back to others.

If ignorance is bliss, buying books is a positive addiction, but still an addiction. If the world seems to overwhelm, then keep it eccentric, like Dylan, like Fellini, like ancient fables—for in this comes freedom. The rhythm of such forgiveness abounds like the sound of Charlie Parker, without his addictions.

Why? Why this move into another part of my life, after all the years at college, Long Island, and in the face of business?

I have seen how much freer you can be when you simply argue with friends like Abe and Winston, rather than wander the malls of the internet to purpose things all day. As with Amazon, Facebook, Google—and the others spiking during this third year of the Virus—2040 is riddled with tales of success that seem counterweights to what I am claiming. In my neighborhood, there are some of us who got there by living this: doing more with less is success. This may prove the opposite of both Allison and Tony. This may be an ancient truth: if you go back to look at the guardian at the gate of Boshazkey, you will find the finest relief sculpture of ancient civilizations. And this gate is an emblem of competitive frugality. If you move stones that last, it takes a focused efficient frugal use of human gesture and talent.

Even with this frugality, once in the gate, you can see stone reliefs that have lasted centuries of jugglers and acrobats. You can have fun while running with competitive frugality. This is my home. This is what I've earned, every inch of it.

To murder one's memory is freedom

Abe reports: much in life is like street jive, all the absurd clacks and clicks plead with you—and with your neighbors—to buy that flashing thing before you. Meanwhile, Earth—that big blue marble in the sky—has been rolled by these storms, like a marble you cannot stop except by stopping to buy. You cannot pay too much attention to this predicament, however, without going insane. This morning, reflecting on the safe grandeur of my home's splendid isolation, I wrote in my journal a few countercultural banners:

Wealth is in the Commonwealth

Wealth is a Social Blessing

Wealth is not in what you own or buy or need

My banners, in essence, echo a protest song: You should not lean so forward in the saddle of your everyday that the horses carrying you can make you fall off, right on your ass, or worse, your head! Wealth is a buffer of social grace.

Now it is true that monetary wealth has allowed me to be a born-again consumer, filling shelves with books and art artifacts and DVDs. I do not invest in Winston's nudes, however. They do not serve him, in his excess, as visual deterrents. He will not eat horsemeat, but he will pretty much eat anything else, wear anything fancy, and be "above" the crowd. The events of your day can be centered in your home, on a deep listening of the nature that surrounds, and the friends that inform.

For free, we look at the large maples in our neighborhood. They are magnificent, like exquisite music. For free, you can smell and recall the grandeur of a Stone Church nearby, already built in 1826. If you concentrate, you can smell that history in your nostrils, and smile. Those great days in the neighborhood remain in our memories. For free. If we forget the constant bombardment of today, we can be free.

I took many walks these days, trying to release my feelings about the trials of Uncle Finn. I took many walks trying to liberate my near future in this time of the Virus. There is a velocity to aging that brings us closer to the eternal, if we wait for it. The bullet trains of doubt only blind us. Look up, look up at the tallest parts of the oaks, and be free.

Suddenly, you feel the bond between neighbors. You are like a faucet, like Uncle Finn, rich with wonder, not things. These absences become the events of our disciplined days: it is the lack of the click of another purchase that stands out.

The objects of our interior life—our best thoughts, and our keen observations—become valued as we age. Thought is an object, and being objective means being free. In our gestures and our conversations, we become like Ben Franklin all over again. We make meaning by defying the very things that caused Climate Change, and the Consolidation of a Few Great Nations. We can retreat to our own neighborhood Walden Pond—it, too, has polliwogs and butterflies, and wombat-sized dragonflies—all for free. And we have many ways of saying to the neighborhood: "THIS IS MY HOME."

It took me nearly a quarter-century of living in this home to get into this space.

We all have high points in our life, what Wallace Stevens, the poet and insurance executive, called "moments of sudden rightness." For Varlissima, it is the sighting of a rare bird that makes her month. For Colette, it is solving the medical puzzle of a new patient. For me, it is people—despite the secrecies that dominate our days. Throughout most of my life, the discovery of another interesting person was my moment of sudden rightness. I found that relationships themselves were like jazz on a Sunday afternoon: all rhythm and joy.

With Varlissima at Home

Driving back north to our home near the Stone Church, I had time to remap those special people in my life. It was like cramming for a big test, flipping through the panels and papers of my memories, person by person, a fine feast. And all this for free, without much to own except the meaning in relationships.

Remapping is a tool-assisted process, invented in Moscow some years back. The remapping protocols allow an exact recollection of friendships, by using the Cloud and AI to download a series of pictures from your shared past.

It is an astonishingly fast process. All you need to do is click the friend function (if you have already uploaded a photo of them on your device) and the period of time you wish to recall. You do not even need to name them, and boom, in seconds, you have a sequence of images from the past that you took of them.

If you buy the advanced features, you can get pictures of your friends that you did not take. The "circles of friends and likes" functions wherever pictures were taken from the same day and same neighborhood on other people's devices. This advanced feature downloads those pictures in your histography.

I found that creepy, so I kept the cheaper models. I tend to stick with what feels humane, and shy away from anything that gives me god-like powers. I do not know exactly who in the realms of surveillance capitalism designed these features, but I do not feel them a friend of the people.

Winston said that such devices help him rapidly get to the essence of a person. I said boldly: "You can sew all this up that way, Winston, but some of us will still see the tears."

Now the machines do remake your memory—for human memory is not as accurate as these photo sequences. These photos put together a picture-based logic that implies a pattern that has meaning. You can define a person by the patterns seen in these pictures, and the Event Police do exactly that, too, but with even better machines at their disposal. They place you in time, at places you've long forgotten. It is the shock of recollection that is part of the thrill, and part of the worry.

Will humans ever be able to do things like simple humanistic literary recollection again? Engineers take out the bugs of bridges by reverse engineering before they fall. We do the same for jets and military equipment. In recent years, we have done the same for people's memories. These photo sequences that remap your friendships do other things to your sense of self as well. If you feel alienated from a friend, when you look at the grand picture of the relationship, it is easy to doubt your grudge.

Winston argued relentlessly with his daughter about this matter of human intelligence relative to machine intelligence. Winston was on the side of machine intelligence, and the incredible fault lines of the human imagination. I do not argue with Winston or his fine daughter about any of this. I know the battle will never be fair. I vote for the underdog, the humans.

If I did argue with Winston, I would mention the following. There are a few exceptions in live people, whose memories are impeccable. A pattern of vigilance develops in some people, I have found, where their memories on bitter victories are more accurate than their memories of simple and sweet victories. In a bitter victory, where a star gets hurt in victory, they remember the actual score per quarter and the moves that brought them triumph.

I have found memory faulty when it comes to dissent, in particular.

"There are important exceptions," Winston reminded us. With an air of certainty, he let me know that "some let the streets of their life feast in memory. Others care little for memory. The State gets concerned when people have a surplus of memory, remembering things they should not." It was hard to discern the bull from the shit in those comments, I felt.

Some memory veterans keep the most important relationships in the world in their minds, not in their devices. I knew this to be true.

From work before the pandemic, I got to know Richard, an exceptional former rugby player from the U.K., who became a global executive. He had the authority to represent the composite voice of over 9,600 pharmacists before the Russian and British Aerospace health committees. This was amazing in both reach and impact. He once told me he could recall, without memory devices, a thousand of those 9,600 pharmacists, their phone numbers, and the recent issue they called him about. I got the feeling that he was hired to observe and to report, but I also sense what a superb spy he would have made.

This Richard also ran, informally, but at the same time, access to all the Asian banks through the Hong Kong hub of HSBC, one of the few banks in 2040 capable of exchange between all Eight Nations. In addition, big Richard—at six foot eight—had a private collection of "critical friends" in all eight nations. These provided him cover and a long, wide safety net whenever he travelled in the Big Eight.

Richard's elevation number was the highest I've known. He was so elevated in this current world of event that he felt, deeply, that another world was not possible. He saw the similarities between those from the Balkans and from the Turkish domains, and insisted that we call them all Europa.

Winston's snide comments on Big Richard still stick in my mind: "No one's telomeres are long enough to know that many people in one single life. He must have extended some basic facts through intrigue and indirection."

The combination of that recollection from Winston, plus the fact that Varlissima was driving faster than usual in her pursuit of our home, suddenly annoyed me. For me, and I hope for you, relationships—and the memory of them—form a kind of accomplishment.

This sequence of human-based meanings remains quite different from the memory of our handhelds, which yell "*Buy…Visit…Receive.*" All day long, "*Buy…Visit…Receive, Buy…Visit…Receive.*" You are not really visiting anything by going along with this electronic mantra. Is that friendship?

There is nothing like a real trip down a real road, thinking about friends and real places, not things, to arrive back home.

Like a Dog Returning Home

I thought about Abe, and I thought about Winston. I thought a lot more about Abe, because of his premature death. In thinking about these friends, I realized for once and for all that there is a profound connection in any real sense of time.

"What do you mean by a profound connection?" I could picture Abe asking at a halftime.

"Well, think about it." I would say to Abe. "Here we are in a place, Abe, Stone Church. Right? A sacred place. Well, back in the day when Abe Lincoln was a mere seventeen-year-old strapping stud, this Stone Church neighborhood stood tall. The trees across from my home were small then, but here we look upon the same trees! That special year, by chance, was also the very same year Thomas Jefferson died. How odd, but true. Did you realize that 1826 was the year that Jefferson's friend, former president John Adams, also died—an exact 50 years after they were passionate friends in the revolution? If you live long enough, you realize time connections exist, making our memory special."

Abe, if he were still around, would take in this historic detail with care, as he knew I selected my home with diligence. He would pause and think long enough, in this imagined exchange of love, for me to notice how much hair Abe had lost since college. He kept his stomach muscle strong; but, like me, the hair went to hell.

Then I would say, wanting to make sure he gets it: "Can you see? Can't you see it, Abe! This sense of connecting of time unto itself, why its realization helps one be decent. This is what the Poles chant in victory: *Warto być przyzwoitym!*"

Abe was a Polish Jew. He'd know exactly what I was talking about. "This is exactly what I mean by saying, 'Just try to be decent,'" he would say. "Once you grasp this meaning in how time connects all—and that each of us is granted the ability to reach across time—you can be decent." I can picture Abe, in his profound mode, half serious, half jiving me, saying, "Yes, Yes. Yes, George. 1826 was a special year."

This realization about time connection is missed by youth, and at middle age, when we are often too busy to even consider it. That is why it is so hard to be decent competitors.

I had come to conclude that time itself was special, when you looked at it right. I used to be desperate about time; but now when near a dear friend, or my wife, or my daughter, I have plenty of time. We really do have plenty of time when we are next to beauty, or next to a loved one, or in a surface battle arguing with some lifelong friends.

I hope Abe understood how much he meant to me. I could never know for sure. I could never directly ask him. Abe's passing gave me a sense that my best days were still ahead; and that together with my remaining friends and wife, I could overcome my fears.

Inside the Stone Church

It was a long drive home, but well worth the drive.

As we pulled into our driveway, I asked Varlissima if we could take a peek inside the Stone Church. I am superstitious about returning home, and I like to put a cap on trips by visiting the church.

We had grown accustomed to the smell of the church in recent years. There was some moisture in the basement, which we had tried again and again to seal.

Thank God the fourteen banners that hung in the church were still fine, after that big storm, still hanging proud as if done by Giotto himself. These are banners of respect and decency, the opposite of today's many political banners. These banners in the Church help me choose hope over despair, and truth over lies. Like the Creek, they struck me as sacred.

Here I inspected them, by gently pulling on each with care and tenderness, touching their purple felt.

The first is called **Prudence**, with a woman at an accounting table.

The second is called **Fortitude**, who stands with a sword and a large marble barrier before her. I never knew why they had carved a small, long dog on that marble shield.

The third is lovely, my favorite, **Generosity**, who stands in a smooth robe, smiling, with a look for the needy.

The fourth, called **Justice**, sits on a throne. She has a balance in her hands, and a look of rigor.

The fifth is **Fidelity**. She holds a music score in one hand and a cross in the other.

The sixth is **Caring**. When thinking of care, my mother taught me to say the ancient term *caritas*, which turns out to be a true recurrent force in human nature, one that anthropologists can now measure in even the most remote underdeveloped cultures, far from the electronics of today.

The seventh is **Aspiration** herself, aiming high.

These were the sacred seven, the banners of hope and aspiration. The banners on the other side of the Stone Church were far less flattering. This may explain why most of the congregation sat in the pews facing the Creek during most services. I felt that a bit lopsided, but such is happiness.

The eighth banner is **Despair**, who hangs on a rope, legs free from the ground. There is a red devil by her right shoulder, as if Giotto himself painted it. Despair was perhaps the most vivid of those depicted.

The ninth banner is **Greed**, her pocket bulging with coins, and a small fire at her feet.

The tenth banner is **Infidelity**. You could see it in her inviting face.

The eleventh is **Injustice**, the one figure portrayed by a man, bearded and self-important, and surrounded by servants. He was not a source of joy for many, but helped mitigate rampant lawlessness by being mean and forceful, like a tyrant.

The 12th banner is **Anguish**, depicted as an attractive, long-haired woman baring her breasts. Some might say Anguish's profile and breasts were the reason some young boys kept coming to the church on Sundays.

I remember a long uninterrupted discourse by Uncle Finn, where he recalled these to me behind my home, a distance from the actual church.

Uncle Finn had claimed the 13th banner was a woman slipping on her ass. This was supposed to be, according to Finn, why we need to keep a sense of humor in our life.

The last banner was also untitled, according to both Finn and Winston. It was the strangest of all figures, neither man nor woman, but a large, beast-like figure carrying a club. Finn said it represented the State; Winston suggested it was the club of Justice itself.

Back Home

Back in my den, I took some folders of Abe's work down, to read it in person, in hard copy.

Reading the actual, physical, yellowed newsprint felt better than flashes on a screen. Abe and I had once walked the entire periphery of Trinity College in Dublin, after absorbing the *Book of Kells* display from around AD 800. This was an illuminated copy of the four Gospels on the life of Jesus Christ, along with select ancillary texts. The fame of this Irish treasure rests principally on the supreme artistry of how these texts were so lavishly decorated. You go to any Irish pub or ask any taxi driver and they know of this collection, open to the wandering public, an ultimately unifying book.

I was thankful that Abe, in his infinite impatience, left for several side trips during those two days.

Everything he began to report in his last decade had a positive twist to it. "*Just try to be decent*"—he said that was the key thing, the only thing in fact, to keep before one's memory. He even called a three-year monthly column "Just Try to Be Decent."

I once had a chance to quiz Abe about what would be the opposite of decent. He said when you see the opposite you know it. The opposite of decent is tyranny.

He talked about how Roosevelt tried to win over Stalin with sweet reason to help preserve democracy and peace in the world in the 1940s. During the 1930s, Stalin had murdered, without hesitation, all of Lenin's Politburo. He then exiled Leon Trotsky (whose secretary was a known relative of Abe's forefathers); then killed more than 25 percent of the senior Soviet military officers.

I looked at my handheld. Abe was right: Stalin had killed 1,966 delegates to the Seventeenth Party Congress, 98 of the 139 members of the 1934 Central Committee, 90 percent of all Soviet ambassadors, and two secret police chiefs. All this slaughter was accomplished before our President Roosevelt secured his alliance with Stalin and Churchill.

Abe was himself a great historian, trying to be decent. I miss him daily.

In contrast, Winston steadily upheld what he called "French sophistication" and our alliance-building with the Great Nations. He suggested, by indirection, that Roosevelt was smart to align with such a butcher in history.

Citing proud wordage from de Gaulle and Napoleon, Winston believed in monumental history—the history of great men. While the U.K. and U.S. and the other nations questioned the Great Man or Great Woman theories of history, Winston silently resisted this view. He refused to budge, saying our entire future as a species depended on it.

Winston believed, from Joan of Arc to Napoleon on, you could take a great person view of time, no matter how unfashionable it became in the news, and then defend it. He could defend them all, from Thomas Jefferson on. We have some evidence he believed all of this, because one holiday, he hung a banner outside his kitchen window, as required. It read:

The Big Eight Rule

Step Beyond the Individual.

Enjoy Your Family.

Embrace the Near Future.

At last, I understood what Winston believed. And it was ugly.

The Science of Emotions

I write because I am more in touch with the science of emotions than those who support the State. This can be ugly, even fierce, but it is true. I write about love, laughter, fear, grief, joy—while others try to control it. My life has taught me, by taking so much away, and then by bringing so much joy in my wife and daughter, that we need a sense of proportion to be creatures of dissent. And we need this refined sense of decency to remain free.

Let me be more vivid. I have a picture of me throwing a pint-sized Colette many feet into the air. Her look of utter amazement and trust is priceless. Abe had taken a picture of her while in mid-flight, arms seeking balance, face in total wonder. I never dropped her.

We need this sense of personal prophecy and joy in our lives. We need a celebration of this sense of life, a sportive seriousness, that will carry us as we throw things up. If you are too fearful, you will never throw your only daughter into a joyful sky.

Everyone needs this job, the joy in life, finding that joy, and keeping it safe like your daughter. Yet everyone also needs their personal dreams. I knew the sheriffs from the Event Police were not as perfect as their records claimed, and I suspected that their game of aligning people's surplus memory was a kind of civilizational repression getting out of hand.

I have been mishandled and hassled by police in my youth. Even though I was a star athlete, and neither black nor a minority, they had hassled me enough—taking me from buses to admonish me—that I kept a suspicion of them each time I saw them.

The authorities were capable of a horrid inflation of facts. Each campaign of misinformation solidified acts of discrimination.

I was ready to embrace my near future. In place of process and observation, I would begin to help others find their freedom and their jobs. At the prolonged age of 75, I had achieved that rare union of observation and practice. It was the absurd trial of Uncle Finn, matched with the velocity of the storms and the warm assurances of Varlissima and Colette, that made the captive Noh masks slip from my face. I felt naked, and enraged.

Chapter Eleven:
"All We Need is Hope"

It turns out, to my and Winston's disappointment, that The Champs never did play The Poles.

The disappointment felt like a warm, intimate, sharply etched chamber of thought in my mind. Abe never learned how long they held us in an "entertainment eternity," never letting us land in the game. This was done with tricks—it was a media masquerade—like the figure-eight moves an airliner makes in bad weather, knowing it cannot land. They call this the eternity pattern waiting for foul weather to mellow. This causes me sorrow. When emotions announce themselves this loudly, it is important to listen to them. Humans need to land.

Throughout most of human history ordinary people, in all their range of variety, have wondered if the elites might banish them. Today, we need to worry about the delay or cancellation of the games without any recourse to tribute or triumph. It is all a goddamn joke, this media circus, this gaming with games.

To maintain self-respect in such a world, I have found I depended on resilient friends, a doctor daughter, and a wife of gold. Without them I could get pushed down by cancellations, sales taxes, merchant banks, international fees, estate taxes, and bad digestion. The older you get, the older your obligations. Wealth itself becomes an alligator purse, pulling at your testicles.

It might have helped if I had seen all this earlier, such as during my college days. My wealth snuck up on me like mold in an old basement, and with it, decades of obligations.

Perhaps this explains why you can count me on the optimist side of the human ledger. Despite this testimony of despair, I have always been able to repair. I repair my faults like a carpenter repairs a misshaped window. After the insults of winter or ceaseless relentless rainy days, I dry off.

The carpenter knows hope prevails in the next plank. "All we need is hope" is the mantra to wake a weary neighborhood, despite bursts of rage and indignation.

Despite this hard-earned self-esteem, the canceled games were disturbing. I was not about to stand there silently anymore. I was pissed. The machines take it too far.

By the middle of 2040, the state has become all anticipatory churn, to keep our minds occupied. There is nothing to dwell on, nothing to concentrate on, nothing that relates to more than a self, for a few seconds. This old man has had enough of it.

Before he passed, Abe had written me a final letter, where he said, "I am proud, George, of how you've lived your life, how you explored the pangs of genuine fear some Fridays, and were all cheers by Monday. Like our hero William James, in the act of becoming, you stumbled onto a plateau of good health."

That comment made my life worth living. That was nice to have and to keep.

Yet despite my hopes, the promise of seeing my Poles in 4DTV had never materialized. The excuse: nasty weather. This was something only a Tony could come up with in our neighborhood. I tried to shake it off, reciting my favorite Scottish exemplar of wicked wit:

"Before you judge a man or a woman or a child, walk two miles in their shoes. After that, who cares? They are more than a mile away, and you have their shoes!"

In a way, the leagues running the sports empires did the same thing. And what were we to do: take down the stadiums? What would that accomplish?

This move is what pissed me off the most, like a fourth shot in a Scottish pub. The state employed an attractive Oxford-educated sportscaster—her creaseless collar of light blue made her look like she came off a starship—to announce an endless stream of replays instead of new games. I did not fall for it; and turned her off with annoyance whenever she appeared on the screen. I chose to see her as another elite brute who, while being able to speak in several Romance languages, was still a brute.

Instead of the Champs versus the Poles, I got to watch Michael Jordan play in yellow, in purple, and in red jerseys over the next days.

I got to see "Be Like Mike" shirts at each commercial.

It was excessive. Remakes are increasingly worth less, no matter how much talent they display at first.

In the absence of the championships, we cope. In their displacement, I noticed an increase in local trials, federal offenses, and slanderous claims against our citizens.

We tried to fill the gap with good memories, conversations between friends. I remembered the song by Dylan, where he is describing a lovely woman who wears an Egyptian ring that sparkles as she speaks. Well, she has the power to turn the day into black, too. Dylan warns that you will wind up down on your knees, peeking through a keyhole.

I had come to feel that way about basketball, my lifelong love. You have to see the truth through all the churn. We are living in repressed times.

And you have to do it in a fashion that enables hope.

Nothing rests, not even the dead, in this age of electronics.

Presidents dig up Nazi icons on Facebook. They foment violence, and mobs. They disgust due process with tales of glory of the self.

Survivors indicate in posted videos how they were almost killed.

Yet after a while, it is easier to stay at home.

Each neighborhood is riddled with competitions to have folks get a higher number in the elevation rules. This is the game we substitute. At times it seems as if anything can be posted, from serious hate to idle agitation, anything to attract eyeballs.

During the months after the passing of Abe, I watched a most amazing posting. It was called "The Stairway to Heaven." In this animated show, a well-built sky god from Africa was living next to an old woman, who kept knocking him with her pestle as she pounded away at her yams. I guess she had bad arthritis in both hips, so she swayed awkwardly as she pounded.

The god was used to being fed the best yams while he sat on a throne made of small, perfectly flattened brick stones. Each brick was about three feet by three feet, an amazing feat to honor his dignity, and hunger.

One day, the god got pissed from all this contact, and went up to heaven. His many sons missed him; and began to take apart the throne and place them into a single long stack of stones. They tried to reach him in the clouds. In doing this, they made themselves quite vulnerable, because as the old hag came up to yell at them, she inadvertently hit the stones with her hip, and the entire stack came down, killing her and all the boys. This forced the Africans to devolve into a kind of paganism the Big Eight did not respect any longer.

This African tale brought me some comprehension that there are things about time you can only understand in extreme old age.

The Return of Uncle Finn

But wait.

I keep getting ahead of myself. I forget the sequence of things.

Remember: no sooner did Uncle Finn reappear than Abe passed.

Uncle Finn, on leave from the Shelter he was sent to after the trial, came back as a hooded Uncle Finn. I could not tell, under this fashionable hood, if he was humbled, but I did see new sheets of actual text in his hand. Had he been writing to prepare a new defense? Often crazed citizens do this. It was also possible that they were just additional examples of what I've come to call Finn's "peep art."

To play it safe, I recorded this in the day's journal: "He had been humbled by the entire time downtown. I felt the world of event would have it this way, adjusting Uncle Finn down to size."

We heard from several appointed members of the neighborhood that Uncle Finn had completed his sentence in the Shelter. They had him at first listen to 70 straight hours of different Bob Dylan songs, to see if his mind was sharp enough to fully recover. Uncle Finn could remember most of them. He remembered the complete stanzas of a dozen, and they were not the most famous songs by Dylan.

They then subjected Uncle Finn to a series of judgments made by the State on street art. Was this acceptable? Was this forbidden? They told him about giant waves, as in the story of Atlantis and in the story of Noah. Finn remembered the passages. Finn knew all the Banksy presentations by heart, so he called all of them dissent art—and he was right.

They then asked him about the differences between the early love films of Fellini versus the more indulgent later films like *Roma*. It was hilarious, and refreshening. Once again, Uncle Finn chose right: he liked the former films.

While he sided with the right interpretation with many of these quizzes, it was almost possibly by chance. He carried in his right hand a ball of smoking incense. They wondered if he had a stash of drink somewhere else.

This type of grilling went on for several months.

They began to ask about specific lines from Dylan, such as, "When did Bob refer to a French General in rags? What language did he use when he spoke of Mount Fuji, and the set of giant waves that once topped the mountain top? How does it feel to be without your home, like a complete unknown?" Etc., etc. It was daunting. But the Russians said Uncle Finn would often answer in complete alignment with the State's preferences.

Despite the mental cleansing he had suffered, he still had this incredible recall. There are many humorous posts about this in the neighborhood, all drowning out our loss of Abe. One said: "The return of Finn means there will be another seven nuts in search of a bolt," meaning other crazies might now be ferreted out by the State.

The Trial

But again, I get ahead of myself.

I forget.

I never told you the full story of Finn's trial.

Once it reached its formal phase, there were ten distinct steps. I now record diligently for you the process of his hearing.

They asked Uncle Finn:

1. "Did you know that at the same moment of your alleged misbehavior, exactly in your old prior city of Albany, another once high-ranking Pole got drunk behind his church?"

The question was odd.

As they asked this question, the authorities flashed a picture of a demon god swinging in the air behind Finn's head. They also ran a banner on the bottom of the public screen, advertising: "Playing at our neighborhood movie theatres—*Phantom of Justice*." The State often confused with this multi-valent type of over-assertion.

2. "Yes," Finn replied, eyes blank.

They then asked in the same breath—anticipating his *Yes*, "How does it feel to know this—do you feel as if you committed a wrong? Does knowing the wrongdoing of a colleague in a parallel capital town make you subject to the same wrongdoing?"

Finn looked a bit stunned, so the inquiring official repeated the question this way:

3. "Did you know, Uncle Finn, that we have verified all of this through electronic evidence? That you once played, like a furtive deviant, with short, lovely encounters behind the Church?"

They played the harmonica harmonies of Bob Dylan as they asked this question.

4. "Yes," Finn replied again, this time his eyes even wider.

He and the crowd were amazed that the State could recall these Precision Events of such ancient origin. We had been getting used to stormy seas, and frequent storms in our neighborhood, but such Precision Recall was new.

The public record now shows that once the prosecutor gets on a roll regarding these precision recall questions, there is a feeling of escalation, like in an art rummage sale or formal auction.

"The Event Police have really perfected their game," Varlissima commented, with a stern grimace in her brows. She did not say much during public sessions, but when she did, I knew to listen, and think it through. Like the entry of Robert De Niro in the film *Brazil* many decades ago, Varlissima's entry into my mind mattered, dramatically. There was a carnival knowledge in what she said, both from the role the Sicilian Mafia played in her blood, and from the crass common sense of the moment.

5. "Uncle Finn," the lead judge, dressed with bow tie and perfectly polished black dress shoes, said slowly. "Did you know we can make your mind recall each of those stray girls, their names, the smell of their socks coming off, the sound of their cough when complete?"

That phrase, "We can make your mind recall…," had the tone of Winston behind it.

The judge had a pre-recorded tone in his voice that suggested Uncle Finn was bound to fail, like that friend of young Bob Dylan who got 99 years in Joliet Correctional Center. In fact, the stanzas of this song were being repeated right after the judge's question, as an echo to the question, helping the audience pre-judge the process.

There were also bell boys beginning to hand out popcorn, as the trial come to a close. There was a general feeling of permissiveness as the floodgates of guilt were being projected on Uncle Finn.

6. "No, sir," Finn shouted. "I did not know your Memory Improvement Devices had advanced to that point."

The Dylan music stopped.

The crowd looked eye to eye, nervous, as the judge stretched his large fat flabby arms upward. To win the female vote, as if votes were being counted at all, the screen now showed the procession of Smith College graduates peeing into their professor's graves, with the chant, "When God created man, he had a better idea in then creating women." You could hear some truck traffic behind their claims.

The chair of the committee, leaning forward, was now more aware that the preordained crowd—some reformed Poles and some Champ competitors—were now looking for something consummate. He pointedly asked:

7. "Uncle Finn, did you know that we can fix you right now and here with this MID device?"

Finn paused. He itched his crotch.

Inside, I could hear him asking: "Do I really want to give up the chance to replay all those past events?" He did not want to forget those young girls, their socks, anything about them.

Did he want to exchange all that surplus memory, and turn those lovely Dylan songs off in his mind?

Did he wish for the loss of those moments of personal rightness?

Wait.

Wait.

We all waited.

Before he answered, he scanned the faces of the crowd who had been scheduled to witness this trial, this Downtown Interview.

About 8 of the 14 faces on the jury remained blank; they had not yet clicked approval of the judges' moves. This was strange. It seemed like a stacked jury, since there were no women present who might sympathize with Finn's worldview; and absent that, there were many athletes in the jury. These blank faces were mesmerized by his next answer. The six that showed any emotion suggested: "Go for it Finn, you will feel better."

Finn knew, from his chats at the library in downtown Saratoga, that most Poles answered the last question: "Please proceed."

This is why most Poles that become great athletes are considered competitive—they can focus on the game because they need not focus on past pleasures, or furtive asides. Unlike most athletes, the Poles remained relentlessly wanting to play another game. That is their number one priority, game after game. These Poles are perceived as a debased and powerless order of athlete, but sometimes they did win it all. Uncle Finn was processed like a Pole.

This is why I still believe we can beat the Champs.

After these first steps in the interrogation, Varlissima lamented: "There is always a great deal of Hollywood in these investigations; leading to the inevitable implants." She continued, furtively, speaking quietly in my ear so low I could hardly hear: "Do they think we are fools, forgetting this is all a show? All a sequence, not a discipline. There were once serial killers in the world, now there is a series of these small abuses by the State. They add up."

If anyone could read her hand gestures, they'd know why I loved her. Bold and smart. Smart and kind. Kind and sensible. Pure of heart and mind. Varlissima was a radical, in silence. And she was hoping Uncle Finn would keep "his wild."

Suddenly, the judge was seen on the screen behind Uncle Finn's head, smiling. The judge was sitting with another man who had large incisors; his teeth looking like they were capable of tearing someone—as in the old days—limb from limb.

8. Uncle Finn now wondered within himself: "Yes? *No?*" The judges offered Finn a wicked, sophomoric game with only one choice.

The judges had seen this "citizen wavering" before. There was so much razzle and dazzle before peasants and people that it was hard for them to focus on the judgments before them. For about 13 percent of the interrogated Poles, there was hesitation before they decided. The Neuro Docs did not know why this happened. Genes? They called this "the Polish hope stomp."

One local scientist compared it to stomping on your cigar. "You knew," he said, "that smoking was bad, very bad, for your heart, and that a cigar represented a known harm, yet when they did the deed, they'd stomp with keen pleasure on the edges of the cigar."

This cigar stomping was also evident in Polish women under investigation. There is the famous case of three woman, Tamara Trojananska, Joanna Nizynska, and Agnieszka Polantionwska, who knowing a great deal about being Polish, hesitated over half a day before the judges! They finished their cigars before they announced their decisions to the judge and the crowd. The cigars had less than a half inch stub when extinguished. Tamara won the day, almost smoking ash.

This game of reshuffling a memory sometimes does not work completely with a Pole. A Polish person, after centuries of abuse from the Soviet and the Nazi, can ignore a great deal of State pressure and investigations. And keep hope in what their history books call "Polish essentialism." Being essentially Polish, not American, I knew what these women were talking about during their trial, and I respected them more than their prosecutors.

Watching the Polish sensibility during my youth, I realized this is what adds an element of glee and surprise in how the Poles play basketball, even with damaged knees, and old limbs, and weak hearts. The coaches give them a little gin, and the pain disperses, and soon they are hitting beautiful focused free throws, a dozen in a row. To tank them up with exactly the right balance between the current game and their memories, they can hit from half court. We can be distracted from things like mental torture this way.

At Finn's trial, the oggly-eyed judge went on, in a louder and louder voice:

9. "Sometimes these Poles have too much in their memories to see the big picture. They are distracted, in their surplus memory."

He went on, his voice becoming that of a pastor or professor, full of detailed fury, and some fact:

"In the past—for the Polish peoples—any details about the Russians, amused the Poles. Even today, they delight in stories about Putin's horrific grandson, about how he enjoys mistreating his wife. Their memories are good for nothing," the judge asserted, sternly.

"They live in a simpler immediacy. They are dumb. They are stupid. They lack awareness. After trying again and again, the officials cannot get it all out, like wax in an ear."

We took this as the banter of those that banish, not as truth. These were the words of humans gone afoul, such as when dolphins hit each other in the head, or they send enforcers and recruiters to defeat the weaker pods.

I could relate, in my anger, to some of what this judge was pronouncing. But it was easier to let him make a fool out of himself. He had the air of arrogance about him. You could almost see the steam leaving his forehead and ears.

I have always rooted for the underdog. When Michael Jordan came along, during the middle days of my life, a mere six foot six in a land of giants, he left a lasting impression. I rooted for him at first since he was, in a sense, a skilled relentless underdog, like my Poles.

At that time, there was a general consensus that no one could dominate basketball unless they were "big" men like Russell. Jordan was not ranked high upon recruitment in either college or for the pros.

But as an underdog he brought grace, force, and fascination back into the game. He was an honorary Pole.

My daydreaming was smacked back into the trial by the judge letting out a loud fart. He then said the word "Fibonacci." As if that somehow mattered to the fate of Uncle Finn.

There was a gross harshness in the nine steps of the inquiry so far. It struck me as distant from grace and force, from the fascination of watching Michael Jordan play or Uncle Finn talk. Uncle Finn was becoming a new Jordan in my mind, and the trial underlined the necessity of it. Uncle Finn's stories had huge hands, reaching everywhere. His shooting-off of the mouth was as classically precise, pure, as Jordan's shots on the court.

Uncle Finn never shrunk from big moments, never worried.

Step 10

Eventually, after what seemed like almost 20 minutes, Uncle Finn stood. With a smile of abandon on his face, he declared: *"Please proceed."*

Uncle Finn's voice was firm, unwavering. I felt like I was in a movie, or reading passages when a hero slaps himself in the mirror.

There was no tone of acquiescence in it.

Finn assumed for me and for some others a pattern of nature to his stance. While the State viewed him as part of their monthly headcount, to me he seemed timeless, a racoon at night, a Bob Dylan in protest song, a man of the hour.

The 4D movie screen behind his head showed a set of colossal chiefs— ancient stone chiefs like those found proudly displayed in New Zealand— sitting in a row. This large backdrop meant something fierce, suggesting some ancient justice had been reasserted. They superimposed faces of folks from the crowd onto these stone idols to make it fun, as well. A few were the girls that had won the prizes from the Champs' games. It was surreal.

The applause lasted longer than the usual ten minutes. Although the AI analytics teams had predicted before the process that Finn would yield a *Yes*, the drama was in the timing of the game.

The decision was final. Soon Uncle Finn would have his surplus memory manipulated, with a regulated implant deep in his right temple.

Within an hour of the decision to proceed with an implant, Uncle Finn was evidently calmer.

He sat down, for a change. He took out the old Church violin. His fingers seemed larger, as when an old man emerges from surgery.

He spoke about one injustice that still bothered him. He noted to our neighborhood that of the 1,453 basketball professionals in the Big Eight, almost 41 percent of them received less than $1 million each year in earnings.

This uneven pay was deeply disturbing to Uncle Finn because the average player spends only about 3.7 years in the majors, due to injury or other competitors. He changed the actual way he played the violin to underline this sad set of facts. His fat fingers seemed to fly with grace.

Uncle Finn shared these calculations out loud, like the old mesmerizing Finn we favored. He spoke with no brakes, like he was the best momentum stock out there on the open market—no hesitation, as if the devices were not working at all! Looking across the gathered crowd by the Church, he wanted us to bet on his insight about increasing the pay of the Poles, and the pros in general. He claimed it likely by January of 2041.

Our neighborhood forgave Uncle Finn these small remaining indulgences in freedom, as they chalked it up to a small piece of his excessive memory, regarding his son's likely acceptance to play for the Poles.

"That too will pass," noted Winston. Winston knew the State well enough that I worried he might be right.

There was a saucy buzz about all this in the neighborhood, nonetheless. Perhaps Uncle Finn still had some excess in his memory, they whispered. Abe suggested the trial had failed! Varlissima seconded the thought.

I did not know what to think. Finn asked us to remember, of all things, "the maverick mother who had raised the 20th century politician, the late great Senator John McCain." I searched and rapidly learned about Roberta McCain's 108-year-old life. At age 96 she had travelled the presidential race with her son by her side. She said: "Honey, I have had a dream life. I never did anything I was supposed to do. It was all luck and freedom."

Was Uncle Finn giving a secret message to the women of the neighborhood? In any case, he remained a full-throated pisser.

The Game of Home

To celebrate the return of Uncle Finn to our neighborhood, the Poles added his son to the team as a point guard. This meant they had enough confidence in his play for him to control the passing and the tempo of the game. This was good news to me and to Finn, who was proud of his son. This was a big deal for our neighborhood, as when a grandkid gets to go full pay to Harvard.

Bravo.

We felt this was real progress in the neighborhood. It helped me broaden my appreciation of T.S. Eliot, game theory, and tomorrow's sorrow.

They gave Finn Junior new long shorts, silver ones, with the number 77 on each leg, and that wiggling dog icon on his cap. He had left a nest, ready to fly.

All seemed well again in the neighborhood.

Winston, reading between the lines of this appointment, reminded me that this did not mean much. It was "all spin and win"—what Orwell used to call "double talk," he said. The Poles would never again be allowed to confront their archenemies.

I reminded Winston that in a true democracy, we have no real enemies, only opponents. He sniffled. Winston said he would bet one of his best nudes that Finn's boy would do nothing of consequence. The Celtics, and the Champs, were too elevated to compete with those like the Poles. "Those glory days are over for the Poles," noted Winston, with certainty as weighted as the closing of a bank vault.

By now I knew that only those gifted in the everyday could be mindful of both the material in sport and its supernatural nature.

This new excitement in Finn's son, nonetheless, paid off for most of us. In the neighborhood's psyche, this was an explosive development. I compared it to when Gaugin painted his gaunt and yellow Christ on the cross. Through strong colors and angry lines, some say the painter used his own face to generate the contours of the rendered Christ. In either case, having Uncle Finn's son sign up for basketball was a kind of formal competition and profound crucifixion. I felt it would prove spectacular to watch the poetry and force of his play.

It was exciting to see him practice in the basement of the Church, the full grace of his free throws, his use of his sharp elbows, the twitch of his wrist. Sure, it was still damp down there from the last storm. But these players seemed to excel in basement light. It was entertaining to be able to watch these stubborn teammates play again in the neighborhood. This was the good news in the bad way Uncle Finn had been processed.

Uncle Finn and Creativity Itself

If creativity is like a Zuni snake that wiggles through the lives of those blessed by its lightning, then Uncle Finn was an example of the notion that creativity did not have much to do with the formal education of the elites. I reminded Winston that the entire life quest of William James, our college-day hero, was proof of that. The most creative seem to come out of modest families in time.

The elite schools never wanted to acknowledge that. It was, in a sense, a fundamental black eye in their claims to fame. This reminded me that the most learning I got from my Cornell years was watching Fellini films.

Uncle Finn, in his prime, was like Fellini: pure, and full of play. They were both master storytellers, ringmasters of human dreams, caricaturists, puppeteers. The main and important difference is that Fellini managed to live his life without the constraints of the State, despite the ascent of Fascism in his youth. The most creative remain creative, despite the repressions of the State, the Dream Book, and their immediate families.

Uncle Finn, too, shows me this is possible in the remaining glimmers of my life. Birds of the business world eventually have to leave the nest, and fledge into creativity. If they are lucky, they will not smash as they approach gravity.

Perhaps we had something right in 2040: shorter pieces and micro-bursts got more attention than the longer diatribes. In our lives of endless streaming, two hundred pages of a book seems exceedingly long, no matter now entertaining. Even a well-made two-hour stream-of-consciousness film by Fellini can seem long at times. What else have we lost in this lack of attention besides libido?

Long past were the days of *Paradise Lost* and massive meditations like the ten books of Marcus Aurelius. Aurelius once meant so much to me. I had recited each sentence out loud to my mother in high school. It took full summers to capture his brilliance when I was studying Latin.

But all was a burst, now, all was free and fast and furious—like a car chase. Nothing amounted to much but a big hill of steam dissipating between the beans.

We had not heard the style of Fellini for some time; it is as if the storms took that part out of our life.

The Exception of Bob Dylan

There were still a few things these days that Winston and I could agree on. One was that Bob Dylan songs were good, long and short, a rare exception to the mix before us.

With Uncle Finn and his son around, it was good to have that style— fancy and wonder and pure unadulterated fun—back into our lives.

One day, months after his surgery, I spent five hours talking with Uncle Finn about over 50 Bob Dylan songs. His recall remained entertaining.

I told all of this about Dylan and Uncle Finn to Varlissima. I earned a lovely smile.

Varlissima then noted that I was a cross between Fellini, the painter-in-rage Caravaggio, and a corporate banker. She added a twist, saying, "But if part corporate banker, you'd need to look like Bob Dylan, changing your snake skin every few years." I took this as great praise, reminding her that Abe was the fine painter, not me. I did feel some of the rage in a Caravaggio, but I felt it in words not paintings. And I had my emotions much more under control than Caravaggio, whose emotional turbulence could be felt even after six hundred years!

I spent a few restless nights thinking again about Finn's fantastic visual memory. It seemed to be peaking again. Uncle Finn's memory would meander like those wonderful Fellini scenes. Finn was sensual, and Finn was fundamentally fun.

Now that he was fixed, would Finn prove altered?

I had been told by a neighborhood doctor that when an implant's swelling recedes, in a few months, as the brain heals, certain memories will recede.

This night I put in the Fellini film where Anthony Quinn plays Zampanò, the brutish strongman who enjoys flaunting his power, just like the Event Police. Fellini once noted: "All my films turn upon one idea, that of power meeting justice. There is an effort to show a world without life, characters full of selfishness, people exploiting each other, and, in the middle of all of this, there is always—and especially in any of my films starring my wife Giulietta—a little creature who wants to give love and who lives for love."

I approached midnight thinking Uncle Finn's son was Zampanò, and that Varlissima had become my Giulietta. Cigar in hand, and gin by my side, I slid toward sleep. Right before the sleep arrived, by routine, I put out the cigar.

I had a nightmare that Fellini was not able to produce his three great movies of redemption from 1954 to 1957. Why? Because the State took away his surplus memory! It was enough to wake me up in a jolt, spilling the cigar ash on the bed.

I told Winston about my dream and my worries. He laughed out loud, the bum. Winston never winked at my faults, never. You can give him an A for consistency in our friendship. Ever rigorous, ever the formal inquirer, Winston did not let me nor Varlissima build up delusions of too much grandeur.

This is the way he built his force in the neighborhood, as the memory of Abe receded. Winston got powerful because he was ready to take power, and store it in private with his nudes.

Within a Week

Within a week, Winston and I were ready to move on. What was left to do? Abe was gone. Uncle Finn was settling in; each day brought him less surplus memory. Varlissima was focused mostly on Colette and her husband.

In this neighborhood calm, Winston and I decided to play our favorite legal wicked game. We were missing Abe, but we'd play it for him.

We nicknamed it "The Game of Home." It involved making an informed argument about how we would die. All it took was some Victory gin, and the game got more alluring sip by sip. After a while, you forgot most but the taste of the botanicals.

When we played for Abe, it was easy to guess his demise, as we already knew. We guessed that he would die of starvation: "Oh, how appropriate," I told Winston. "It makes sense that he would slow up due to a deregulation of the sensing and selection of nutrients. He only drank coffee and beer at the end!" We smiled, as if knowing the cause lessened the pain. We also knew that Abe's daughter was ready to thrive with his resources, once gone. As they say in Ireland—God never closes one door without opening another.

"And what will you die from, Winston?" I asked.

He paused, uncertain. Winston did not expect me to ask the question in this sequence, assuming he'd go last. I had at last flabbergasted my college mate. Or maybe the pause elongated the drama of his eventual answer—as if he was in a public trial. Regardless, I insisted that Winston go before me.

Eventually he said: "Stem cell exhaustion." This was hilarious, as he always disbelieved in the resurrection of hope. He added to the declaration: "If there is anything that stem cells represent to life, it is hope." Here he was dead right.

I told him that left the theory of telomere attribution as the source of my anticipated demise.

Winston, nasty at times, recited the Irish proverb at me, saying: "The man who is nearest to the church is not necessarily the holiest. *An te is gierra, don teampall nt he is giorra don altaior.*"

I told him I did not need the famous phrase repeated in Gaelic. Winston liked to show off his Gaelic whenever possible, or his French, but not his inner thoughts. We were drifting more apart in the absence of Abe, his energy the glue between us. I was the one closest to the Church.

Death the Classic Way

Those classic Greek and Roman books we had read during our student days—Winston could cite Cicero on a well-spent life better than most—claimed that how you approached the dignity of death mattered. It is appropriate that old friends return to this theme more frequently as they approach their end.

This was one of the last games available to us at the Stone Church neighborhood, besides basement basketball. It is not a common game in old age homes of the State, nor is it common in most underserved areas of the Big Eight Nations. However, in the well-off rural neighborhoods, where the wealthy could usually live on well past their due time, the tendency for morbid reflection is becoming a more common theme. This is what explains the basic conservative instincts of the old.

Varlissima and I often wondered about the classic claim of dignity in death:

1. Is it not true that death can be a privilege all in its own?
2. In increasingly vivid ways, the defiance of ordinary lifespans that today's medicine brings us serves to distort things.
3. How one dies is far more the great elevator speech than Jefferson's ideas of hard work on the farm.
4. That is why people read the obituaries first, and then go onto the news

Winston, like Thomas Jefferson before him, seemed to advance in life by his abilities to capture complicated ideas, not necessarily by his actual belief in those ideas. Thomas Jefferson expressed many ideals of equality and fraternity, yet had slaves. Jefferson disliked religion; yet after his death, religion was taught again at the University of Virginia, in the open and with some relish!

Winston, in reasserting the masculinity of the State, did not believe in aging. He really did not believe in becoming, even during our first debates about William James and the passage that had first made us friends. He had, like Jefferson, outlived some of his principles in his own life. Winston spoke of freedom from the State, yet helped all statesmen escape the usual taxes. This was a form of death in a classical way: compromised.

One Sunday morning, while rereading Wallace Stevens, I was remembering all the nuances and complications of the judges' ten-step processing of Uncle Finn. As casual flocks of pigeons made sputtering shit over the Church, I thought about the greatness in rephrasing a truth. This is what Winston was a master at in the end, rephrasing what was once a truth.

It was disturbing. It was disgusting, the way Winston and his brethren documented Uncle Finn's use of foreign pornography behind the Church; not to mention the details of why his son threw him out of his house. It was all excessive. And we had to move on.

Those casual flocks of pigeons flying overhead warned of a new storm season in our neighborhood. Winston came over one night, and we took out again the The Game of Home. Even Varlissima joined in, knowing Abe absent. I took out my own best bottle of gin for all three of us.

After a while, Varlissima said, "Let's move on." She wanted to catch up on what rumors were flying around the neighborhood on Uncle Finn's return. He was no longer the talk of town, but he was news.

We all were nearing our end that evening, when a feature of my memory came alive. Perhaps it was the fatigue—we had stayed up much later than was regulated for our age and elevation.

The memory was nothing short of monumental, such as when George Orwell's Winston looks out the window, awaiting his illicit Lucia, and finds a square Norma-like woman, singing happily, singing naively, as she hangs the wide, white diapers of her babies on the line. In Orwell's world, this moment of a person singing free of the State, of sudden rightness, means everything to the reader.

My late-night memory began with a song from 2020, when Willie Nelson was still alive. I could picture the old bard vividly, humming the song with his special twang, about a grown man going back to his mother to ask her what his father said right.

This grey-bearded country singer got it right when he sang a song. The song made me cry, even after all these years. The older I got, the more penetrating it felt.

There is a scene in the song where, as a boy, whenever he was hurt, his father would pick him up and "kiss the hurt away." This is the part of the Willie Nelson song that made me cry. I never had a chance to remember my father lifting me. I am sure he did it. I am certain he did it. I can feel those lost moments with my missing father. I was with him for my first 1,000 days on earth—when you calculate it. But I never really remember it—that gentle lift in a father's hands—the gentle peck to the forehead.

This song kept working on my nerves, making me grow in my appreciation of missing persons.

The gin was once again getting deeper into my brain. I could not tell, and did not care, if I was hosting Winston properly. I felt a rage at the mob that had fixed Uncle Finn.

This complex of emotions made me feel a bit out of character, but the hell with it. Throughout my career, during any descent into a social error, or during any time when I detected deceit in the Event Police, I relived the deep feelings of this forgiving song. It, like this pure unadulterated memory, helped me survive for another fight. Memory can be an accomplishment, besides a rich, turbulent source of renewal.

All we really need—besides a good wife, keen friends, a fine neighborhood, a sense of humor, and a rich shelf of fine books—is hope.

Chapter Twelve:
"Let Us All Start Again"

You may have thought by now that my story would be over. But you would be wrong. Yet, I guess I was also wrong, and have grown. I do not want you to be wrong.

You must wait a bit to realize how much more Varlissima means to me, beyond her bubble gum lips, her wide teeth, her skyscraper brows, and her Sicilian wonderland. You must wait to realize the power in my daughter. You must wait, as I wait to die.

All those banners about "Tyranny is Tomorrow" are wrong. Only the creative self is real. Machines do not make our memory. WE DO. That should be the only banner that reigns high over our heads: WE DO.

A Return to Vivid Dreaming and Vivid Writing

I have given you a sense of how my vivid dreaming, that deep sea of sleep, has helped me twist from repression.

One's freedom remained tied to how well you allow and enable your vivid dreaming. That exists deeper than your job description, even deeper than your family and friends. Vivid dreaming, when converted into daily disciplines, like writing and thinking, can help you twist off the salty blankets of the State, and start again. With vivid dreaming, your name can mean soup meat, you can be your origins, and more. That is the miracle in life. God is good. God is love, and you celebrate these truths through rumination.

Abe, even some 20 years ago, wisely noted: "Dreams use our heads like our wives used our body! Why do I say that? Well, think it through. Dreams procreate your future, one more rich and more diverse than a simple self."

This was life-changing for me, like that first alert by William James that a life worth living is about becoming. Abe called this high fact a sportive phrase: he called it "moving through family beyond the blame of self." This proves more ancient and lasting than even Dracula.

Winston saw in our last years a "surprising set of solutions that can help incorporate the world." But for me, it was sleep and my wife that made me free. In sleep, my vivid dreams liberate, reshape, and surprise—in that order!

In the end, the only way to defy our destinies is to be creative, to keep the machines and the State guessing—at both your personal genius and your particular take on the light desserts and sweet unexpected turns of each day. The Event Police cannot quite tabulate you. "Even Popeye and Santa Claus knew that," the cynical Winston chimes in from a much earlier conversation. In my mind, they all resonate.

Tony, and other the warriors of the State, cannot fully monitor the creative things we are born with, if we chose to cultivate them. I chose writing over tyranny to get the record straight. Thousands do this each generation.

Here is how I want my tale, my fable, to end for you. I want you to consider these ways to beat back tyranny in your lives:

1. They make eye contact and small talk with all, including stray neighbors like Uncle Finn and the Event Police.
2. They keep a private handwritten journal series; and a public persona through their publications and neighborhood conversations.
3. They investigate rather than simply download.

4. They keep this private life amongst family and a tight set of friends, sharing it, cultivating it. Nothing is accepted as received from the State without this deliberation.

5. They have an informed enemies list, as they believe in the truth. They know a light heart lives a long time, too.

6. They let some of their thoughts stand out, to keep the memory devices busy, as they take responsibility.

7. They defend the institutions worth defending, like libraries and churches and other forms of spiritual life, even when they are banned from them. You can be a believer and embrace science, health, and the good will of others.

8. They are patriots of the world, not simply obedient servants of the Big Eight Nations. They foster civil disobedience, like those rural Italian towns over the ages.

9. They even, like Tony, can become armed, but in a far more reflective way. They do not do it for the State.

10. They believe in social value, family, and friends.

These ten principles were the ways I now choose to live my life. Like a famous Irish proverb found in the scraps of Uncle Finn, company with these people and these principles shortens the journey. I am talking about you creating your most precious life.

These ten principles are my equivalents to the banners in the Stone Church. Mine have been made more personalized by my lived experiences. I knew some of this all along; perhaps we are born with glimmers of these guardian principles from the start. Yet it is through daily rumination that these principles are enacted in a life as real to your family and friends and readers.

But you really need to earn your scraps of expression day by day. There may appear to be a masterful over-arching sense to this neighborhood;

but it's only through the storms of your own phrasing that you settle into something that makes sense for you.

What Matters is Mindfulness

My concluding advice can be thought of this way: "Defy the machines. Start keeping your freedom journal."

This helps reduce your dependence on Victory gin. It takes that crown of thorns off the top of your spine, and parks it on a shelf. Each piece of your own writing earns attention, like those magical beads of 21st-century Japan called *ojime*.

As you aged in Japan, and matured into a self both known and unknown, you decorated yourself with *ojime*, *netsuke*, and *sagemono*.

Do you know what I am talking about?

Can you visualize these small Japanese miracle objects?

These are carved spirits in whale bone and precious ivory, which allowed you to differentiate your kimono, the daily dress, with function and force in Japan. Each piece embodies values and principles, both of craftsmanship and valor. Everyone in Japan remains human, wearing these objects, but everyone has their creativity upfront through these decorations. In Japan, there is a quiet, subtle serenity, an intertwining of function with decoration—as in good writing.

I thought of writing each day like that, determining what *ojime*, *netsuke*, and *sagemono* the day deserves. Abe went for the news; I went for the shape of the day. There are other means of liberation that await your experimentation: music, friends, good conversation. Yet it is the miracle of writing that gives one the confidence to fly.

The ancient scrolls and records show this as well: The average reader is fascinated with detailed, open writing—always has been, always will be, despite changing tastes and the currents of popular niches. They even like the open, less disciplined fashion in which an Uncle Finn provides scraps and stray comments.

This approach to writing allows a mindfulness that keeps us alert to change. This helps the Japanese be calm when the unthinkable arrives at their island estates—like large Americans or brash Germans. Rabbis and priests and holy women through time suggest this as well, in their stray prayers, left behind for us like Uncle Finn's fine warnings.

The Magical Clan of Writers

After a short morning of writing, I would sometimes smoke a cigar. Forgive me. They are fun and furious, like a well-phrased sentence. This too was mindful. Each puff came with a ritual attentiveness, as I watched the winds of change drift the smoke from my nostrils.

Cigar-smoking can be like memoir-writing, making meanings from the smoke of your experiences.

It does not matter if you are white or black, male or female, educated or self-informed; you can use your creativity to sit under the trees of life, find some shade, and make meaning.

Once you do, you can hear Mozart's *Requiem* without fear; you can walk to the Church to look afresh at those banners; you can run with the times and not be of the time.

You can be young while old, and full of joy during days of repression and hurt. This is the great quest.

This was our way for centuries—the magical clan of writers, the troubadours of old—even after the State confirmed alcohol and smoking bad for society.

In ancient Japan, you would carry our tobacco in a small leather pouch, much like Abe's notebook on the weather. These pouches were often articulated, for man and woman, with porcelain or ivory *netsuke*—one being a tiny skull, another being a shell made into a bird. There were plenty of frogs and orbs.

I can imagine an entire universe that withstood the passages of time, as many of these artifacts were hundreds of years old by the time a relative used them again. Good things last; only hate and ignorance expire.

These became in Japan the memory devices of a good family. The royalty did these in ivory and whale bone; the others—the Japanese equivalent of Poles—displayed the same creativity in porcelain. All were creative, all were expressive this way in their profound observant quietude.

When I roamed the streets and neighborhoods of Japan in the 2030s, before the travel bans, I sensed most people, all citizens in Japan, were of the same level, equal in beauty and hope. Like a cat, the citizens of Japan knew how to purr for their own purposes, while achieving comprehensive social cohesion. This was their social eternity, in contrast to the constant battles over properties and memories now dominating the Big Eight Nations. There was also a sameness that would never work in Stone Church Road under the current regime of things.

Yet I could be free to imagine these days in Japan. The real beauty of writing is not that writers get the last laugh on the conventions of history. Sure, that is true; in the end, when push comes to shove, any book—even a badly written one—has more clout than an electronic device. But it is the writer's life that matters, the fact that they can beautifully reshape their life story into different essences. And that they give the world the books, recording all this as they depart.

We are all born one way, we all have a *Natura*, but you can become a dog if you wish it as a writer. Each book in a sense lets you start all over again. You can make darkness visible, fears virtues, through the entire rig and tag of storytelling.

"That is the real beauty in the act of writing," Abe once said, despite the oath of accuracy journalists keep. "It is a freedom on the march. This forms a song-like recording of what you see, a moment in time hovering with your feelings. Time and consistent expression mix like soil into an earthy sensibility, a voice that lasts, when you are free to shape things."

Life goes on. The words remain fixed on the page. As things swirl, you can go back to the words, back to the passages of your own old and new testimonials, but with abundant humility and calm.

When the machines churn our souls like a tornado, we misunderstand each other. Gone are the days of broad consensus. Yet in writing we prevail. I am fond of this memory of agreement with Abe.

It matters that many feel this way about writing. Abe and I were kindred souls in the end.

A Finale

When Tony made it eye to eye with me, I was prepared. I knew that Tony would come back to our neighborhood to finish what he had started, complete monitoring.

From my first dinner with Tony and Allison, I knew I had to prepare for an eventual face-off. For his return, I had put on my favorite Zuni belt buckle, a demonic icon. This metal belt was possibly a thousand years old (as the Zuni had survived in Southwest regions for that long). The silver belt consisted simply of a well-proportioned bear, eye and ears carefully demarcated in the metal. Knowing Tony would be armed with assault weapons, as well as the latest surveillance gadgets, I knew I needed an ancient counterpoint.

What protected my pride and my contained rage was simple: there was a lightning bolt that traveled like a ditch through the mouth of this Zuni belt buckle, in a snake-like curve, out of the bear's asshole. I had heard that conspiratorialists have clan codes about what to trust and what to fear. This Zuni belt buckle means, essentially, *"Give up or Drop your Shit."* These conspiratorialists never knew what to capitalize, or what to spell.

Standing before Tony at last, I had a heart attack.

I had a heart attack, big deal, tens of thousands have them.

While there have been many advances in prevention and treatment over the years, by 2040, heart attacks are more common than cancer and dementia. This I found both hilarious and liberating.

You have to ask why. Is it the stress of the Event Police, of the State itself? Or the pandemics of the internet that come and go monthly now, weakening our resolve? You know. And you know now how to resist.

Somewhere in the world, at any given time, we are experiencing very bad weather. The media makes us all isolate from it, as if it will dominate our neighborhood. Fear and more fear. Yet being mindful erases the fears.

Being an ex-athlete, I want to demonstrate the event process in my heart for you, both before the attack and in the weeks after, in case it matters. For in this episode, I sense both a finale and a coda.

First off, remember that when your heart is faulty, avoid simple decongestants like Advil and Sudafed. These things are as common as ice cream, advertised after every storm, as if they were the Savior's solution to all our problems. Be free of that which corrupts your chances of recovery.

In fact, if you have heart failure, even on step one of the five-step process approved by the State, you should avoid all nonsteroidal anti-inflammatory drugs. Simple as that.

I do not wish to exaggerate and say that this always works. Nothing will make a racehorse out of a donkey. If you have a shit heart, as Winston used to say when his favorite player missed a free throw, you'd make a shit racehorse. But if you are ordinary, like me, you have a chance of avoiding overmedication.

In that moment, I felt like telling Tony all this about his heart—right in his face. Except I was the one having the heart attack.

I was still in what they call the advancing process of the attack. I mean I had already had the heart attack, the heart had already jerked into deep stress, and Tony was staring down on me like a bloody boxer above his prey. But survival is not based so much on the attack itself, as in what you do during and immediately after that attack. Remember that, and flourish.

"No use crying over spilled milk," my mother used to moan. Now I knew what she meant. You have to move on, get past the initial stages of the heart attack. You can hear this in the most momentous movements in Brahms and Mozart. Move on.

Abe once said, after surviving his first heart attack, "Heart failure is like divorce. It is frustrating! It is more problem than solution. There is good news in the bad news," he said, ever optimistic. I loved Abe, I fondly remembered during the first spasms of my heart.

Why was I thinking about Abe, in these moments of deep stress? Because I love Abe. I love what he has brought my life since college.

But there, on the ground, outside the Church, I did not really care about how he outlasted his three heart attacks in his 50s, when I am turning in pain on the ground. I know I cannot serve two masters, the memory of Abe and my heart attack process. I stopped thinking about Abe.

The pain was convulsing my legs. It felt like the worst muscle pull I've ever had, as if a 7-footer during my basketball days ran his elbow full steam into my chest.

I felt a bit confused, agitated really. Famous proverbs rushed through my brain. What's rare is wonderful. It is often a person's mouth that broke his head. God never closed one door without opening another.

The thought of God eased my soul. Every time I returned to a positive phrase I calmed a bit; but as in childbirth, there are convulsions.

I thought of that day, now years ago, when Abe told me about the "good news" in heart failure. I remember asking him: "Give me an example," and he said "Go look it up yourself!" Damn it, I never did look it up!

Wait.

Wait. A great deal was running through my brain now. The thought worth repeating reemerged to the top of my fog, like a prayer: God never closed a door. This gave me an opening.

Suddenly, I remembered my favorite places, visited with Varlissima and the young Colette. Ravenna, Italy—her astounding stonework and art. Eton, where George Orwell and a stream of dissenting intellectuals were grown under the good meals and shadow of the King. We loved our visits to Edinburgh, a most sacred place, full of festivals and good cheer. And Sterling, and Dublin and Belfast, and Sydney and Melbourne—they all raced through my mind now. Each place I remembered relaxed the chambers of my ailing heart.

As I relaxed, I visualized a beetle's sturdy secret. I once read in *Science News*, in an attempt to impress my daughter while she was in medical school, that there is a diabolical, ironclad beetle whose exoskeleton is so tough you can run over it with a small car, and it survives. My visual memory displayed his dark black unbreakable exoskeleton as a flash before my mind; and then I saw the cross-sections of the insides—as if I were once again a student of insects in college studying to meet a stupid medical candidate distribution requirement in the pure sciences.

While some of my lifelong friends always thought about the worms at the core of human life, it was somehow fitting that my essentially Polish worldview saw the answer in a beetle.

This *Phloeodes diabolicus* can survive crushing situations 39,000 times its own body weight. Zipperlike ridges connect the exoskeleton's robust knobbed top to damage-resistant ridges. The bottom half of his body, where all the vital organs reside, are thereby protected. The trick is that on its sides there are jigsaw puzzle pieces that, when squashed, form a protein glue that holds together the damaged parts. Those repaired fractures then help the joint absorb further impacts, as he walks through his life.

This memory gave me the strength to proceed, to see what mattered next in my search for balance from the harm intended by Tony to our neighborhood.

"Well," I said. "*Yerk*! You are a *YERK*, Tony," I thought now. The arrogant Tony refused to give me a hand. He was the furthest thing from a guardian angel.

In my frantic mind, I next had a vision of my daughter. In this desperate place, squirming before Tony, I imagined a young Colette, having convinced a military police soldier to put his machine gun down, frisking the cop to see if he has a notepad she can use to draw on! The cop, in playful obedience, raises his hand across the wall and spreads his legs.

I was getting a distance on Tony overhead. I was giggling, to his surprise and to the surprise of the Event Police inching near. As further solace, Bob Dylan songs started replaying in my mind, never a feeble mind, despite the host of basketball related surgeries—twelve in total so far. I hear his

Harmonica
It started like a jazz piece, but then turned

Folk.

I felt a man, listening.

I feel everything now.

Dylan makes me into a child man again, a man.

A full-grown man is not a lonely man, with his

Music that reminds me of things majestic and surviving.

Everything about Tony had this high-tech angle to it.

Was he taking my pulse remotely?

Did he have a hidden monitor that was calculating my chances, as he stood above me? Fuck off, I thought of telling Tony. Go back to your militant machines!

The Dylan music drove like a drone into the sweet riffs of a Muddy Waters guitar. I was flying above Muddy's original Mississippi slave shack, now, looking down where he was born, dark as night. A man from the Library of Congress found him, a white man, and you could see deep delight in Muddy's face as the man used his back trunk to record Muddy, right there by the shack. It made all shake and shimmy, even a white boy like me. I was feeling much better thinking about music instead of Tony, that bastard.

I then heard Varlissima's boldest family member tell me in my face: "You are not Daddy material." I felt a twinge near fatal; but the music came back to this Polish idiot from near the railroad tracks of Long Island. I could not sing the blues, but I could use my brain and God's will to get out of a shithole, like Muddy did.

I pushed Tony away when at last he tried to lift me up, having read a few Heart Diatribes. These were daily downloads sent by the State to anyone over 60. Most simply deleted them unread, but I was earnest enough to read some of them. These helpful diatribes made one thing clear: You should not let any agitating people handle you if you are having a heart attack.

During a past visit to my fine, gentle Greek cardiologist, Dr. Spanos, he had confirmed this. It was not merely State propaganda. With Tony now near, I could only recall the negatives in my experiences with Tony, and I said: "Stay away you—fraud!"

This brought me back to my original first impression of Tony, as a man holding his wife's ear like a wolf.

The anger left me as I lay on the ground, and I was beginning to feel better. I stopped sweating, turned to my side, still feeling weak. There was a heaviness to my limbs. My legs were no longer jolting. I did not know what I was talking about. I had no proof of fraud, nor did the Event Police. Tony had returned to the neighborhood to take care of Uncle Finn, not me. Yet I felt vindicated in telling him to shit off.

Tony looked at me as if it was my fault for having this heart attack. "What a jerk! What a jerk!" I kept thinking, until I remembered it was important to calm down, think about the beaches you loved. Think about each of the people you love. Think Ravenna, think Colette, think of the lovely decades with my wife. Think about the gifts my mother brought my life.

When I had slowed my breath through a kind of meditative discipline and pride, and could speak again, I found I had nothing left to say to Tony. In short, I said, knowing the Event Police near: "There are many reasons we have overworked hearts. Mine is only mildly overworked. Ha! I will send you an emoji." Again, the long sweet longevity of Japan was entering this writer's soul.

Tony kept staring at me, looking puzzled. At this point, Allison got out of her truck. She looked mighty fine to me, more slender in fact than ever before. And in leaving Tony's side, I felt she was that wolf. Sleek, free of the bully. Like a good neighbor, she rushed to get Varlissima.

The three young Event Police stood there, with their electronic notebooks, clicking away for the record. A gentleman cop, a black man I remembered from a speeding ticket long ago, assumed the role of a guardian angel over me, his face turned yellow as his wide grin took on the glow of a smiley face.

Despite the deep breathing, I was hallucinating about the smiley faced cop. I could swear by the seat of my pants that he had white angel wings, and that his black face had turned into a yellow smiley face.

Tony stared roundly at me. He had also had a heart attack this year. His bleaker attack peaked while he was heading fast into town on his motorcycle one rainy Sunday. He slid on the stone pavements in the rain, and the ambulance got him to the emergency room "just in time."

Tony's heart attack was ten months before. He had left our neighborhood to recover secretly from a heart attack that humbled him; which worsened on his motorbike in his new town in Maine. It was a miserable recovery for him, like salt in the wounds of his pride. As soon as he could, thinking himself fully recovered, he rushed back to our town in revenge.

My thought patterns included…word patterns, the image of that rope with the large mass descending, images of lovely Colette's face with her gift fox and the camera, her athletic form serving a volleyball when only ten, the slender grace of Varlissima through the decades, my home, the Stone Church, the latest breakthrough the Cleveland Clinic found in 2040 regarding one's heart. It was a stream of blood in a sense, not thoughts. My body was concentrating the resources of my brain to serve the needs of my overactive heart.

"Amazing," Tony said, as if he were hearing my thoughts. "He is not dead yet, Allison."

Varlissima arrived; she was always so strong.

She lay down next to me, face to face, her lovely Sicilian eyebrows in a massive sympathetic knit. I began instantly to feel better. Tony asked, "How the hell did he do that?" I had no clue, really. I simply survived. Abe, if he were there, would have said it was a recovery based on the good will of all my friends, and all the good books I had read in life.

The Event Police had not seen such a recovery in years. One of the three cops said out loud: "I am beginning to learn to mind my own business." The smiley cop radiated good charm.

To my surprise, it turns out heart failure patients who are heavier and have slightly higher blood pressure actually do better than thinner peers like Tony. You need a little fat, a little buffer, to survive these late day seizures. It is true after all, I have proven more tenacious than hunger itself. You needed to be like me to weather the storm.

Tony had always been tall and thin and anxious, like so many of his peers in the elite teams. He was buff, thin as a rail; but he was also always anxious, never calm, never satisfied.

In studying many bankers and CEOs, I had seen that many times in the elite class. They looked emaciated. In Polish essentialism, we take some extra tummy to be healthy. I was always rounder, despite the daily exercise. I was always laid back. I could fall into a nap any time of day, not because I was tired, just because I knew how to relax. Bankers went for cocaine. I rented a couch.

I began to laugh inside!

Varlissima actually sensed I was laughing inside.

She put her warm hand on my forehead and smiled. I began to smile openly on the ground. There was some kind of divine justice in all this that even George Orwell had not conceived. I felt like I was in a Fellini movie, one of the nicer, kinder, shorter ones. I was all eyes and ears and feeling, and calmer too.

"Is it not cool that you can re-synchronize the heart after all that coffee! All that excess! All those fears, all that literary tension!" noted an admiring Winston, who had just arrived in a brown sweater and tie. His arrival gave me further strength.

In the end, when Tony came back with a vengeance, the only thing that could save the neighborhood from his wrongful wrath was his weakened heart. He had the guns, he had the equipment, the night scopes, the records, he had the conspiratorial theories and evidence. He simply did not have the heart to go after me.

And Tony never got enough sleep, keeping up with the other conspiratorialists deep into each night. That shortage of sleep might be the real killer.

It was clear to me that he was worse off, far worse. I sat up, looking at my wife and friends. Sitting up across from the Church, I felt the good support of its entire history. The neighborhood wanted me to survive. This gave me and the extended neighborhood great pleasure.

A Fellini Finale

Progress and power matter

A week later, feeling great again, I prepared tombstones for my friends. After a scare with my heart, it pays to get your papers together. Your circle of loved ones and friends probably saw it all coming, but you never have enough time to honor those friends in public.

This was the new sportive tradition of 2040. You could post your tombstone banner before everyone else started chatting about you at your death. You extended your life by recording a message about your own death, before your death. This gave you a chance to shape the discussions, getting ahead of the cluttered chatter cycle. You can shape your own tombstone, before the Event Police and State officials get at it. It was modern, available to all, and electronically sound.

Here is what I came up with for my closest friends and myself. They let me change Abe's tombstone banner from "A Good Journalist" to:

A good boy, a faithful father

For Winston it said:

A good tax attorney

For me it said:

A good dog

I thought it necessary to end our lives with a sense of humor, humility, and good cheer. Most dignified people in 2040 strive to come up with a personal banner and fail. They come up with State-based drivel, nothing creative. They say stupid things, like "President, CEO, Chief of This or That." They are still wearing their Noh masks.

In 2040, the ability to come up with a clever, crisp slogan for the billions of citizens out there is a very rare achievement. Yet it is attainable, if you work the chatter and machines right. Few, a very few, almost one per neighborhood, can die with celebration in their last few hundred memory entries.

"That is the scheme of things," Abe used to say, tilting his head like a Hindu Brahmin and shaking it slightly, in a ritualistic fashion, from side to side. If Abe had been a good boy, then he was like the African cultures he admired during the days he lived and worked in Harlem, before retiring up at Stone Church. "A gross generalization" he would say to me, but still, in essence, a truth.

The deceased Abe was a good boy, according to the machines of memory now tabulated rapidly by AI. Like many in Harlem, he knew how to serve the community, how to give as well as take, and he knew that the Event Police were not on his side. He was not selfish; he was genuinely a very good boy. This makes me smile. His authenticity outlasted the chatter. Abe deserved the tombstone I proposed, as it was based on a generous general truth.

In some ways this was parallel to how the legends of Robert the Bruce were made in rural Scotland in 1306, or how the legends of Robin Hood prevailed for centuries. It is the people that bring the brand forward.

For our times, legends were earned, and shaped. Each proposal had to come with an appendix of solid data to pass the authorities. For Abe, a 9.7 on the Moody scale, a 9.9 on the Standard and Poor's scale, and a perfect 10 on Fitch. Those were Abe's scores regarding his "goodness" to society. He had good credit, in society, you have to admit. (It is plain dumb to dispute the aggregators.) How much more can I say? A solid, well-educated, Jewish journalist of some generosity and soul, Abe was my dearest friend, besides my wife.

Now when it came to our tax attorney, Winston, who helped the State's elites dodge taxes, you had more trouble verifying his genetics and his aggregated self as French. Legends are stabilized through relational analytics. If you have shit relations—only with the rich and the State—the people can smell it.

Winston was, without a doubt, partially of French descent—about 48.3 percent of his cells, upon old age, were still discernibly French. "I have some attributes of being French," he said, "but if you look at how I morphed my genes by becoming a universal Big Eight tax attorney, it would be wrong-headed to characterize me as associated exclusively with French culture." The memory devices did not dispute this, and allowed me to file the tombstone papers that would eventually put TAX ATTORNEY properly on this stone. I could not get anything more revealing, anything about his ability to persuade or to delight. I found him a great friend, but the machines did not, even though he spent a life supporting those machines.

Despite this elaborate mixing of human genetics, some of the products of human culture last rather long. Some find this in words, others in Japanese artifacts, and some in buildings. Legends live long, while most of us cease. In rare places like Ravenna, you get them all preserved for centuries in one place. I felt that way about my home. Whatever happens to me, the home will stand tall alongside the Church.

Having sealed up the tombstones of both Abe and Winston, I retired to my home library. There is nothing better than being a dog at home. I could feel my invisible tail wagging. I took down a big picture book from our last trip to Ravenna. This incredible archaeological treasure seemed, unlike so many places, to withstand all foul weather, all foul murders, everything intact.

For the full 1,600 years that Ravenna was in triumph, as the happy capital of the Western Roman Empire, it was sacred. The picture from my library wall always brought this memory back to me: Varlissima and Colette and Colette's family spent a week together—with fine Italian pastries in hand—roaming around Ravenna. I remember the joy in Colette's daughter's face when she stood near Dante's Tomb. Varlissima loved the Arian

Baptistery. I was fond of the Archbishop's chapel—and the sacred Palace of Theodoric back before the last pandemic.

On this trip we discovered something even more amazing than the famous Byzantine mosaics. About three meters below the street level, we discovered a set of forgotten tombstones.

In this isolated area, the most striking building is a stately Byzantine home, dating back to the beginning of the 6th century, when most of Europa was in the dark. This home alone had fourteen rooms, and three courtyards; and the third chamber, whose tombstone was busted, remained unnamed. It was the tombstone of someone worth remembering; but the place of magnitude had assumed it.

We found this mesmerizing. And here it was in Ravenna, near Dante's tomb archway! The entire home was decorated with polychromatic mosaic floors and marble inlays of great and careful craftsmanship. There were several hundred square feet of colorful inlaid mosaics, with geometric interlacing, floral and animal figurative scenes of dancing wolves, and stern-looking locals. We had stood there in a kind of family eternity, eyeing the place, called "Dance of the Four Seasons." This remained the happiest moment of my life. To be with extended family, in the great succession halls of Ravenna. The trip gave us a feeling of the great succession called history.

Returning from that family vacation, at last able to travel again, I reserved a resting place for Varlissima and myself right in our neighborhood, behind the Church, facing the Creek.

I managed to hold back the tears. It was no longer fashionable to visit grave sites, nor churches, in 2040. But I argued that no one knew what 2050 or the storms of 2060 would bring, so a few of us were allowed this benign tradition.

Despite all the fabulous AI machines of 2040, it remains damn hard to discern the exact roots of culture in any deceased person. There is some whiplash in the numbers. For time itself underlines a fact deeper than all our family fantasies: We are all from a complex blend of tribes and mixed neighborhoods, a discernibly mixed hybrid now of other cultures.

Last year, for example, Enrico Fellini was found to be more Polish Jew than Italian. This undermines the desperate desire to establish family dynasties. The mix is what matters, not the family masks.

It is possible, for example, by Colette's generation that she will prove less than half Polish. It was evident in the whiteness of her skin, in contrast to the southern Italian skin of her mother. Varlissima has a darker, more oil-blessed skin than Colette, yet Colette had a firm mix of her Eastern European features as well. Such is the mystery and mix of succession, and it is a blessing when humans can see this.

The bullet train of change itself seems to kill the idea of a single originating culture anymore. That is why in the end, both Prejudice and Tyranny are dead. In fact, I may not be 100 percent Pole in the end. Let's settle it this way: "Winston was a good tax attorney."

The future is damn anti-climactic.

The future of most lives is so elongated, so intertwined, our memories never die. But when it comes to Tony and me, there is always change. There will be centuries of debate over who was right, and who was wrong. That is the way it should be. The Champs and the Poles should be able to compete, in a matrix and mobius strip of time.

As for me, the long-living Varlissima will have the final word. Or does that rest in the dose response of our lively and lovely Colette?

The End

Saratoga Springs, New York
March 2021

Author's Note on the Birth of *2040*

Writing is an exercise in self-discovery. After watching a world of readers respond to my more than a dozen books since my 1990 first Simon and Schuster book, I can say you can reinvent yourselves through this self-discovery.

That is the miracle.

The business of book publishing, on the other hand, is an experiment in social guesswork. What does the public want next? In between churns a world of creative indigestion. Hey, hold up both hands now, turn around, and read many other good books.

Think about these original genre books—*Animal Farm, 1984*, Ray Bradbury's *Fahrenheit 451*—did they take off right away?

No, but readers knew they were in for a special ride from the start. Did librarians call these works fables, or fabulous, or furious instances of science fiction? Most readers, like the university teachers, took time to calibrate their surprise, which brought them delight, entertainment, and persuasive concerns about the near future they explored. These now-classic titles did not make full sense from the start, nor were they meant to do that.

This book aspires to do the same for you. You may laugh, as you cry. That is OK. The book before you is multi-purposed, shocking, raw. Full of rumination, like a fable, yet also thoughtful action, twists to a plot that now surrounds you in your computing every day. Event and thought, thought and event—the things of your friends, roommates, and loved ones, too. Why did I write it this way?

One day, while talking with my literary agent of five books, I paused, asking myself, do I still need agents? He said, regarding George Orwell, that in his first career as a publisher, his publishing house purchased the rights to the mass market paperback edition of *1984*. In the late 1970s his house collectively sold approximately 250,000 copies a year. Not bad. But in 1983, this agent led a management-leveraged buy-out of the publishing house. His Board's timing was excellent. *1984* sold 2,000,000 copies in 1984. Orwell had already been dead four decades, but the social guesswork paid off for Bob and his firm. It took that long to click. Now 70 years after Blair's actual life, I read his seventh biography while writing *2040*, and realized he was aflame since Eton.

There was a historic lesson in all this. I had learned—in running my consulting firm for 40 years—how to make money and not let the money make me. And there is a larger lesson: luck counts more.

This got me thinking. I had written a *New York Times* best seller, *Doing More with Less*, as an homage to Ben Franklin, when big Ben was already dead for three centuries. That title brought me, to my surprise and delight, large consulting clients, including a four-year gig for Walmart serving their expansions for food supply chains in Africa, an extended assignment working for Toyota on competitive frugality, and a strong, stern, science-based assignment building a council of advisors for firms like Merck, Walgreens Alliance Boots, and bp to fortify their future. I did not write this book, or any of my books, to make more money. In life, I was a provider out of instinct, not grand plans.

My imagination is not that managed. It is more full-throated and free-wheeling, and I work to keep it that way, writing each morning. The books simply come out. So, I thought, why not follow as best I could the agent's good fortune in getting Orwell alive by writing a homage to my neighborhood, and the challenges it faces? After a dozen books on business and society, why not a fable on society and business, twisted into the year 2040? This was not fantasy. It was paying respect.

Now 66, I have the time to write something completely new. Covid-19 helped as well—my usual three or four client trips per month came to a standstill. Across ten months I had time to draft these chapters, again with the superb editorial advice of Peter Lynch, and the guidance of early readers, some noted in the endorsements.

I wanted to explore how an individual becomes free in a repressive society, where the machines keep our memories and edit them. Despite our daily bombardment of messages from our computers and TVs, I find human behavior eloquent—desiring each morn to be free. But what if every tiny thing we do in a neighborhood gets reviewed, evaluated, and processed—like meat after its slaughter? What happens when my typing on a computer is accumulated by machines and sold as testimony of our behavior? By 2040, I anticipate this becoming a key feature of identity, of becoming. This is very different from a mere 40 years ago, when three college mates, George, Winston, and Abe, met.

Forty years later, I am still running my management consulting firm, but it is now easier to sequester time away to write. I was listening to a great deal of Bob Dylan—his wicked wit resonated during this viral pandemic. I was also reading Shoshana Zuboff's new book titled *Surveillance Capitalism*. Although a beast of a book to get through, her scholarly book still stuck with me. I have read another 40 books on failures in our intelligence agencies since 2016. "Somebody has to do something about this!" I yelled in my head.

The idea that companies scan our clicks, gather the debris of our book orders on Amazon, record every damn Google and Bing search we do, and then sell that information as a predictor of our next purchases? That makes everybody's ordinary day worse than Jack Nicholson's in *The Shining*. That was worse, far worse, than Big Brother watching overhead, since these were an endless stream of tiny ants inside our thoughts, squirrelling around inside our computers and hand-held devices.

You may think I am exaggerating, but that's the rub.

Normal, everyday corporate surveillance is now worse because this prying involves personal liberties impacting everyone on Earth. From Africa to Manhattan, anyone who did their daily clicks was being accumulated. It involved choice, personal choice, the essence of becoming; and it now involved a simple new bite at the apple on the Tree of Knowledge. This mean-spirited, machine-accumulating, emotional discovery for me was like experiencing the shock of a new Fellini movie. I planned to provide a finale that surprised as it entertained.

This caused me to remember a very strange dinner I had in my neighborhood with an electrical engineer and his former literary agent wife. These nice-enough people proved to be conspiratorialists, certain the world would go crazy and that our streets would soon be unsafe.

Suddenly, almost in one dream, I saw this book, about what is freedom and what is fate in a neighborhood like my own, here in Saratoga Springs, where people are people and friends are friends, but the whole world seems in chaos over social unrest, police brutality, and surveillance. It even became a book about domestic bliss. I could explore the stern freedom that independent thought and writing enable over the fierce and furious worlds of event. Thus, *2040* was born.

About the Author

Bruce Piasecki has written 16 books since his 1990 Simon and Schuster book. A few have gone into several languages. Right now, he is trying his hand at different styles of writing—fables, novellas, dramatic scenes, folk tales—and he is bringing his old favorite books down to guide him during this pandemic.

Here is why he wrote this eighteenth book, mostly in 2020.

To outsmart this feeling of Viral captivity. To mock, with dissent, the State's dictates of fate. To rediscover the true meaning of friendship. To express love of his wife and daughter. To leave a mark on this electronic wrinkle in his computer's ceaseless updating in time. To strive, to dream, to do it again the next day. Amen.